ROAD KILL

ROAD KILL

Jack Ketchum

HEADLINE

First published in 1994
by HEADLINE BOOK PUBLISHING

10 9 8 7 6 5 4 3 2 1

British Library Cataloguing in Publication Data

Ketchum, Jack
Road Kill
I. Title
823.54 [F]

ISBN 0-7472-1066-7

Typeset by
CBS, Felixstowe, Suffolk

Printed and bound in Great Britain by
Mackays of Chatham PLC, Chatham, Kent

HEADLINE BOOK PUBLISHING
A division of Hodder Headline PLC
338 Euston Road
London NW1 3BH

*To Paula White
in the land of her druthers*

SOLANGE: When slaves love one another it's not love.
CLAIRE: No, but it's just as serious.

Jean Genet
THE MAIDS

By and by the judge rose and moved away on some obscure mission and after a while someone asked the expriest if it were true that at one time there had been two moons in the sky and the expriest eyed the false moon above them and said that it may well have been so. But certainly the wise high God in his dismay at the proliferation of lunacy on this earth must have wetted a thumb and leaned down out of the abyss and pinched it hissing into extinction. And could he find some alter means by which the birds could mend their paths in the darkness he might have done with this one too.

Cormac McCarthy
BLOOD MERIDIAN

PREFACE

It was newly summer.

Rule drove 89 North toward Waterbury.

The proof that it was summer was his windshield. Mosquitoes, flies, bees, midges, mayflies, moths – their bodies left a thin white paste across the glass studded with harder parts, with wings and mandibles and antennae, with pollen baskets and compound eyes.

It's amazing, he thought. You can't even move in the world without hurting something.

Every step.

Something's disaster.

The highway ahead of him was the trajectory of a bullet. Rule was riding in its jacket. Its nose was his windshield.

Hurtling through the living summer air.

THURSDAY

One

Rain again. Rain every day this week. The air in the bedroom so swollen by moisture that his hands felt sticky, his body sticky, the sheets as damp as if he had just made long and passionate love to her when in fact he hadn't touched her.

'We've got to talk,' Lee said. 'Carole?'

She shook her head. 'Not now.'

He watched her lying there staring up at the ceiling, wrapped tight in the sheet, her bare long arms crossed over her chest. The cats on the floor beside her darting suddenly out of the room, chasing each other, disappearing down the dark paneled hallway and thumping down the stairs, their claws skittering on the highly polished wood. He heard one of them hit a banister and keep on running. Then a piece of furniture below.

Some other time they'd have laughed listening to them banging around down there, playing.

But like she said – Not Now.

He saw the tightness in her mouth prematurely aging her, giving him a view of her ten years older.

'We've got to talk about it,' Lee said. 'You know we do.'

She started to cry. The tears rolled down so suddenly it was as though they'd been waiting in ambush for her.

'There's got to be some other way,' she said. 'I can't do this.'

'What other way? You tell me. Tell me something we haven't tried already.'

Her sobs like soft explosions. They shook the bed.

He reached over and held her. He knew that holding her couldn't count for much. That they had come to a place where none of the familiar gestures seemed to work anymore, not even the most basic, where their pleasures all seemed poisoned and their attempts to touch subverted.

My God, he thought. *Look what the man has done.* He'd never have thought it possible. That now he had to will himself to feel for her when once it had been so easy.

He held her anyway.

* * *

7

His embrace barely reached her. Barely got through.

Inside her images seethed and wrangled. The man Lee lying next to her wasn't part of them. They were all images of her and Howard. Howard and her.

Standing together by the sea at Rockport, his promise to protect her made against a vast flat wall of sea and sky.

Then the bed. This bed. Her arms and legs tied to this bed. Howard getting off her saying, Don't worry, I'm not going to kill you, I'm taking off the gag. I'm not going to kill you this time.

Their first Christmas after the wedding. Close your eyes. Go on. Go ahead. Now open them. *And Beastie just a tiny kitten – so small she fit in the palm of your hand – peering out confused and startled over the bright red rim of the stocking, and Carole knowing that this was permanent, that she was happy.*

Howard standing on the lawn at four in the morning. Raving. Then handcuffed, furious inside the squad car. The policeman Rule with his tiny nub of pencil licking it staring at her bruised swollen face and writing in his pad.

Skiing the Alpine Double at Mount Haggarty and Carole so unsure of herself, her first time, his consideration of her total, focused. Knees bent, all right? Use the poles. *She had never felt so secure in all her life.*

The sound and feel of a blade drifting over her skin. Don't move. Don't move and I won't cut you.

Howard passed out drunk. Pissing the bed. And Carole waking, aware of the sudden spreading seeping wetness, changing the sheets first thing in the morning so that when he finished his shower it would seem as though it had never happened and he would not be embarrassed nor would she.

The point of the knife moving down across her belly into her pubic hair. Maybe I'll shave you. *Smiling.*

The arms around her pulled her tight toward the body that was not Howard's, that was thinner and smaller than Howard's and did not smell of bourbon or gin or Ralph Lauren Polo Crest or hot fresh urine.

'I can do it,' Lee said. 'You just get him there.'

Her face and neck were wet with tears. Apparently she had stopped crying.

'You trust me, don't you?' he said.

She looked at him and nodded. When in fact she trusted no one. Not really.

For a moment the silence seemed to beat the air above her with invisible wings, she could feel them drift away from her through the evening damp. A vanishing. A flight of souls.

She had never felt so lonely.

8

SATURDAY

Two

There were times Susan thought, who is this *alien* here beside me?

Now, for instance. They were nearly all the way up the gentler face at Smuggler's Notch, nearly to the pond, their path surrounded by maples, mostly — but you could smell the pine and fir trees perched along the cliffsides. It was a beautiful clear July day — one of the first really good days of the season with all the rain they'd been having. They were together.

And Wayne was scowling. Hardly talking to her.

That damned fence, she thought.

It's the fence again. You want to bet?

She doubted that there was another soul in Barstow who had one like it. White birch pickets ten feet tall and hung so tightly together around his pitiful angular cheese-wedge half-acre of land that hardly a sliver of light slipped through on a sunny day. You could stand on the lawn at ten in the morning and imagine being eaten by a shadowy row of teeth.

Teeth that were ten feet tall.

All to keep out the neighbor's dog. According to Wayne.

She'd laughed at first, saying why in the world do you need this? but she had to admit that he'd done a good job on it really. Very meticulous and even admirable in a way. Even if she still could see no reason for it. Even if it did look like a miniature Fort Apache, almost dwarfing the boxy old GI-bill home he'd inherited from his mom.

The only problem was that the neighborhood kids kept raiding it, tearing the slats off, stealing them while he worked nights. He'd had to replace three or four of them so far. Or was it five?

Wayne suspected the Leigh kids two doors down. But he had no proof. And seemed to spend half his time lately brooding on it.

When here you had this *day*!

The path wound around the side of the mountain. It opened up into a clearing. Tough windblown grass growing thick and short and hardscrabble rocky earth. Down the cliff-face through a stand of poplar (*shitwood* Wayne called it, because it threw no heat) you could see where they'd just come from. It was a ten-minute walk from here — though the straight vertical drop made it seem a whole lot closer.

'Let's rest awhile, okay?' she said.

'Why? We're almost there.'

'Just for a while.'

It was cool up here now that they'd stopped. Her blouse was soaked in back and she could feel the dampness along the waist of her jeans. The gentle even breeze felt wonderful to her.

'Okay,' he grunted.

Well God, thanks a lot, she thought.

He slipped off the backpack and tossed it down. Never mind that he'd probably just mushed the sandwiches. He sat down on a chunk of granite, kicking absently at the dirt in front of him.

You'd think he'd make some effort, she thought. With him working nights at the Black Locust Tavern and her working days at Mountain Lodge they hardly even saw one another lately except on weekends – and weekends had been lousy through most of June. Even the Fourth of July had been rainy. Hadn't he ever heard of – what was it? – *seize the day*?

There were times she'd actually considered marrying Wayne if he ever got round to asking. It was still kind of early in their relationship for that but it seemed like a pretty good idea sometimes. She'd be out of Woolcott at least.

She'd think of that. Then she'd consider how *dark* he could get sometimes, what an unreachable pain in the butt he could be.

She didn't know.

Probably, she thought, he should have sold the house after his mother died and gone elsewhere. The neighbors all seemed to irritate him now. Maybe there were too many memories in that place. Too many familiar faces. Too many kids he'd grown up with who, like him, seemed stuck there.

They'd met in his bar. It was just three days after his mother's funeral, he told her. She was amazed he was even working.

She remembered later helping him go through the house, the sheer incredible *poignancy* of things in a life that death had interrupted. The newly-washed curtains waiting to be hung. The social security check marking her place in the Agatha Christie novel she'd been reading – the book was almost finished. The stuffed lobster wrapped in foil awaiting some special occasion in the freezer.

According to Wayne, her favorite food.

And it seemed so terribly *wrong* somehow that this woman, whom she'd never even met, would never get to hang those curtains, never cash her check or finish the novel or get to taste that lobster, that she'd had to let Wayne get on with it alone for a while – while she went out into the yard and had herself a good cry.

12

It occurred to her that a life was only measured time, really, and that you were the only measure. Like people were all just a bunch of clocks each set to a different time, each fatally winding down. And that seemed to her so sad, so lonely.

It's *got* to be depressing for him, she thought. Living all alone there. It's got to be. It's still only four months now. You don't just dump thirty years of memories overnight.

That's why he's still this way, she thought.

This broody.

That, and maybe the Driving While Intoxicated rap. The poor guy couldn't even *drive* anymore.

It was costing him a fortune in cabfare.

She thought, I've never seen him cry. Not once.

Well, she wasn't going to let him get her down. Not today. Not with this beautiful day here. Not with this clean fresh air and the warm sun and gentle breeze.

She knew a way to cheer him up. If only for a little while.

They were all alone up here, nobody around. And it was the perfect day for it too.

A little adventure could go a long, long way.

'Hey Wayne?' she said.

He looked up at her, expressionless.

She smiled at him anyhow.

She pulled the blouse out of her jeans and felt the cool breeze slide across her belly as she started in on the buttons.

The breeze tickled, made her giggle.

She unzipped the jeans and walked over.

It was the worst it had ever been.

He had her on the ground. Had her naked. He had her legs spread wide and he was sticking it into her and it was hurting her all right, she had her blouse down under her but that wasn't doing much, he could see by the expression on her face that she was part all excited and part unhappy with all these pebbles and rocks and shit grinding up through the grass into the pale flesh of her ass – so he poked at her harder, let her have his weight each time. He wanted her to hurt, to bleed a little, he wanted her shoulders to bleed and her back to bleed. Wanted her ass to bleed. He wanted . . .

. . . *anything* that would get rid of this tension that started in the muscles of his back, ran up through his neck and roared like a freight train through his brain, that seemed to kick chunks of brain-matter out like gravel through his ears, his nose, his eyes . . .

Jesus!

13

It was the *worst*. It was always the worst every goddamn time. But this was the *worst*.

The absolute killer.

The pain didn't matter.

There were so many things to think of that the pain was only one of them, inconsequential. The breadth of him inside her, the feeling of fullness there, the taste of his sweat on her lips and the dark hair curling wavelike down his forearms, his lean good looks tensed now and straining and the smell of him and what they talked about sometimes when they talked about his hopes and dreams for the future because he wasn't much of a bartender, he knew that, he wasn't that great with people and he wanted to buy his own place – and her dreams too when he would let her speak about them, about kids and family and a house somewhere that was not his mother's house but somewhere in Barstow not Woolcott, a life with a future. There was plenty to think about.

So she didn't mind the pain.

Not at first.

She felt his hand clutch her breast and began to ride the pulses happening inside her as the hand travelled slowly to her neck and clenched there, his fingers curling, strong, cutting off her breath a little and then a lot, so that he had her gasping – *and she came*! Came suddenly and so unexpectedly under him that it startled her, his fingers sinking deeper and it was impossible to breathe now, *impossible* – and my God what was he *doing*? – terminating her orgasm as instantly as it had hit her and filling her with a sudden strange kind of wonder looking up at him, because the face that was so intent on her was also as distant as a straight-A student dissecting a frog in a lab – and she felt an icy terror.

Wayne? *Wayne?*

Death a real, sudden possibility, a comet streaking across her suddenly gone-black-as-midnight sky.

She struggled, clawed at the fingers sunk too deep for her to grip and stared up into his face pleading at him with her eyes, aware of her tongue protruding eyes bulging blood soaring through her cheeks. She twisted under him and kicked and pulled desperately, hopelessly at his forearms, stones raking her spine, she pounded him with her fists, trying to scream but nothing but a bubbling strangled sound like something under water coming out of her until the curled hard fingers seemed to receive some distant message, some caution from the brain – and he released her. And she could almost breathe again through throat and lungs that throbbed with rushing life as he groaned and collapsed on top of her.

He rolled away. Lay panting while she gasped and fought for air.

14

And being next to him was like lying next to a poisonous, treacherous snake. She got to her hands and knees and scuttled away.

'You *bastard*! You fucking *bastard*!'

'I . . .'

There was no way to know when the tears had begun but now all of a sudden she could hardly see. She wiped her nose with the back of her hand and groped for her blouse, her panties, her jeans.

'Bastard!'

She stumbled getting into the jeans and nearly fell, still dizzy and sobbing, too much movement too soon after . . . what had happened . . . and him just sitting there watching.

Not moving. Not reaching for his clothes. Just sitting there looking dazed.

Looking almost . . . my God! Looking almost innocent!

'You *bastard*! You almost *killed* me! Was that your idea of some kind of *game*? Are you *crazy*?'

'Susan, I . . .'

'What? You're sorry? Is that what you're going to say to me? You're *sorry*?' She shook her head. 'Jesus! and to think that I . . . Jesus, *I'm* the one who's crazy!'

'Susan just listen to me, all right? I don't know what . . .'

'*NO*, you bastard! I'm *not* going to listen to you! You come *near* me and I swear I'll kill you. You understand me? GOD DAMN YOU!'

She couldn't stop sobbing. Chest heaving huge deep still-liquid gulps of air. Still so out of control of herself that it hurt.

He reached for his clothes. She wiped her eyes and watched him.

She saw no remorse. No concern for her.

He doesn't care! she thought. My God. He really doesn't care!

And the tears this time were worse in a way than before because they came from somewhere deeper inside her. Not from lingering fear or pain or even anger, but from the loss of him, the loss of her idea of him and of the two of them together. She had held that idea much closer than she'd imagined.

'I *loved* you,' she said. 'I can't believe this. I can't believe you would do . . . *this* to me. I think you need help or something, Wayne. I think you're a . . . very sick person.'

She buttoned her blouse and tucked it in. Turned. Her footsteps along the stone and dirt path unnaturally loud in her ears as she stumbled toward home down the mountain.

He'd come so close this time.

In the end, he hadn't dared.

God! he'd wanted to. Every cell and nerve-end in his body seemed to demand it of him. Its power was wonderful, the holding back a brute physical ache. And now he felt drained, as though pummeled by some massive orgasm. When in fact his own had been weak, brief, unfulfilling. Nothing to what it would have been, he knew, had he given in.

Had he killed her.

He wondered – for maybe the thousandth goddamn time in his adult life – why he hadn't dared.

So close.

He tied his Reeboks, got up and slipped the backpack over his shoulder. He felt depressed. It would be good to walk for a while. There was a place down by the pond he thought was okay. He had the sandwiches.

Jesus! She'd been angry!

Thinking about it now, it was almost comical. He almost laughed. Because of all she didn't know. Because of what none of them knew and what they couldn't see.

That so many of them *asked* to die. Men, women, kids. Their sex didn't matter. Their age didn't matter. The Leigh kids who kept tearing up his fence at night. Roberts, the fatass next door with his goddamn dog from hell. Half – no, nearly *all* – his regular customers over at the Black Locust Tavern. Murdoch with his smelly backyard barbecue every summer. The weird old lady who waved to him from her three-wheel bike and whose name he didn't know but who seemed to know him or want to know him, some friend of his mother's maybe attempting some fucked-up down-home intimacy.

Assholes. Going through life with so little on their minds that it was comical. Knowing nothing *about* life, really – that life had nothing to do with love and home, family and friends, that life was made up of stealth and planning and *brains*, brains and guts and will. That, and the obvious – the isolation. All of them thinking that they actually mattered to somebody. And that because of that their weasely little lives had to matter too. When they didn't. Couldn't. Ever.

He kept a notepad and jotted down offenses. 'Roberts: dogshit in left-hand corner of the yard, 1/3/93 – he picked up the big chunks but left some smeared on the grass. *RETAL.*' Or, 'Loden: ordered scotch with water back, then tells me no, *soda* back, 2/25/93. *RETAL.*'

Just so he wouldn't forget just who and when.

He wondered why he hadn't.

Killed her.

It felt cowardly somehow.

There had been deaths at his hands for sure but he hadn't dared for years now, not with what they called the higher animals, and even then it was only

16

cats. And one old miserable stray dog.

Even then it was wonderful.

Of course the aftermath wasn't. Not exactly. He'd had to bury them in his yard. Worrying all the time that his mother would see or suspect something. Whereas here, now . . .

Here he could have just pulled her into the bushes and left her that way.

The way God left His dead.

The bird who strikes the wire.

The old racoon too crippled to fish or scavenge anymore.

The weak and the stillborn and the cold and hungry.

The way the dead had been left useless – no, not useless, because you had to think about the soil and how the dead enriched the soil – since life began.

God's way.

There was nobody who would miss her. Not for a few days at least and maybe not for a long time. Her parents had moved to South Carolina and they'd never been close.

They had that much in common, at least, he and Susan. Nobody would miss either of them.

He lit a Camel. Susan didn't like him to smoke. Now it hardly mattered.

The Black Locust Tavern had gone half smokeless three months ago. A separate section, and smaller than the other, for those with the habit. It was a case of the manager, Peters, allowing himself to get pussywhipped by a bunch of yuppies and blue-hair oldsters.

Peters was in the notebook, naturally.

RETAL.

He climbed a shelf of rock and allowed himself a glance over the edge. He was susceptible to vertigo sometimes but felt sure that this was the way to beat it. Just keep on looking over. The trail below was obscured by a squat stand of windblown pines growing out of the rock, trunks twisted like elbow joints of gutter pipe to accommodate the need for growth both out and up simultaneously. The pines weren't doing too great a job at either. They looked small and beat and scruffy.

He moved away. The pond wasn't far.

He had dreamed last night that he and his mother had driven to a house neither of them knew but which was to be her home from then on and he abandoned her there, old and crippled in the legs, which she had never been, left her standing shaky in the enormous open yard looking confused and frightened and angry. There were cats in the yard and she hated cats. He had driven away laughing. The dream was very vivid. Very real.

He wondered if Susan would ever fuck him again. It was possible. But not likely.

17

Too bad. She was pretty good at fucking and there were fewer notes about her in his notepad than there were on most people. He decided to give it a week or so and then see if maybe he could talk to her. If he could talk to her then he could possibly convince her to start fucking again because even if it wasn't the whole thing it was something.

He was considering taking one of the sandwiches out of the backpack, unwrapping it and eating it along the trail because he'd worked up an appetite by then with all this *stress* when he heard voices – shouts – coming from below. He walked over to the edge again and peered down through the trees.

He saw movement there, shifted to a more open area and saw the three of them clearly in a tight little circle moving in and then outward, back and forth like a rough awkward dance slightly off the trail in the brush.

He felt a tingling. Something scuttling crabwise down his spine.

He saw what they were doing and forgot all about Susan and all about his notepad and the dream of his mother and all about his sandwich. He knew suddenly that his life had changed forever and he let it flow over him.

He watched.

Between the first and second strokes of the Louisville Slugger, Howard Gardner had time to entertain a number of notions, think a number of thoughts – none of them too deep but most of them important.

You little bitch you're not gonna get me was the first thought and probably the most significant. Because that gave him anger, and anger gave him fight.

Wrong! I'm gonna get *you* was the second most important simply because it was so utterly wrongheaded. His immediate concern was the man with the baseball bat. Not the woman. At the moment the woman was just a distraction. And that was too bad, because Howard did not need any distractions.

Move and tuck, he thought. *Come on. You can get this guy. You're bleeding, dammit!* He could feel it rolling down the side of his face. *Fuck it! Get the bastard. You've got the reach and you've got the weight.*

I'll kill the little bitch.

He should have known in the first place.

Something was wrong with the whole setup. Why in hell would she want to be alone with him after all this time, and alone in the woods, no less. For what? Old times' sake? Because they used to climb up here and picnic once in a while? Those days were long gone and since then she'd taken the house from him and the car and half the business and even had the Barstow PD on his ass, had a restraining order out against him the little fuck so that he wasn't even supposed to come near her, his own ex-wife! But there was no restraining him then – no way – and there was no restraining him now.

The dizziness wasn't good, though.

The guy Lee had been standing behind him. He'd never even seen the guy. Carole'd simply stopped to admire the scenery and suddenly bam! lights bursting in his head but Lee had misjudged the reach. Caught him midway through the wood instead of at the thick end of the bat so that it slid off his ear and the side of his head down to the collarbone. The collarbone felt broken. But Howard was standing. He was by God standing!

He feinted left and came in right, beneath the blow – boxing the guy, just like in the Navy. Planted a right fist in a surprisingly tight belly while the bat rolled harmlessly off his shoulder. The guy fell back into the bushes and Carole made a choked-off screaming sound behind him. Some woman-scared little shriek.

You bitch.

You fuck me, and then you fuck with *me and now you want to get rid of me. Is that it?*

What's the matter?

Am I too much trouble for you?

He turned to her, to maybe (quite fucking *possibly*) throw her the hell off the mountain – he could do it, they were that close to the edge right here – and he was wondering if he would *feel* like doing it to her when he got over there because it was *completely up to him*, it had always been up to him whatever he wanted to do with her, stepping toward her thinking oh to hell with it, to hell with the running after her and the hassle and jerking her around, trying to make her life fucking miserable, it would be easier just to end her nasty little life right here and now, he was thinking this when the guy got up out of the bushes and let him have it again.

He'd screwed up bad, turning toward her. Going after her.

And the guy was good this time. Much better. His head split open really bleeding now so that he had to wipe the blood pouring down off his forehead out of his eyes in order to see, and he realized that he was on his knees. He didn't remember falling.

But something was queer. Something was wrong. *What the hell was happening?*

The guy should have hit him again by now.

Sure. That was it.

What the hell was wrong with the guy?

The guy had *hesitated*.

Asshole.

His vision cleared enough to see a pair of legs standing in front of him and he grabbed them, jerked them toward him and hugged tight and lifted and Lee fell, flailing at him with the bat, smashing down across the middle of his back to his hip, the bat coming down so hard that he could feel the hipbone crack. Not like the head-wound. Hell the head-wound hardly hurt at all. Pain like a bulldozer now.

But by then he was up on top of him pounding at the blurry oval that he knew was Carole's lover's face, watching it turn red suddenly, red with the guy's blood or his own he wasn't sure which and didn't care because he was connecting, he could feel teeth jab into his fist and then something soft that was probably his eye and he was howling, Howard was howling dousing his pain with blind ecstatic glee of manslaughter when he sensed – not saw – her step up right beside them standing above them and sensed – not saw – her lift the rock.

He smelled the new fresh dirt off the rock. It smelled like the blood-smell only richer. Thicker.

And then for a moment he felt some kind of amorphous contact, some sudden enormous pressure from above snapping down his head and his neck, Lee sliding off to one side, the earth and grass looming.

And then felt nothing at all.

Wayne lay low over the rocks. No vertigo now.

No.

He couldn't believe what he was seeing.

They fucking *dared*!

He almost felt like shouting, like whooping up there in sheer delight. My God! At first he hadn't been sure what he was seeing, it had looked like maybe nothing more than a fight down there, maybe over the woman. One of the men had a baseball bat but he'd seen worse in the parking-lots of bars at night with jacks and tire irons so that it was only at the end of it when the woman picked up the rock and brought it down on the taller, bigger man that Wayne knew what he was seeing.

Murder.

He felt like calling down to them. *Hey, guys! Hey! Include me in!* He felt like going down there. See this thing up close. Hell – maybe even help out a little. Who the hell *were* these people? Where the hell did they come from? He couldn't *remember* being this excited. Not by anything! He was aware of his heart racing and a pounding in his ears.

They *dared*!

God *damn*! he wanted to go down there.

But instead he did the smart thing, he guessed it was the smart thing, he watched silently as the man wiped the blood off his face – he was bleeding from the mouth – and then bent down and lifted off the rock. The rock was big and flat and beneath it the man's head looked like somebody had pushed it all out of shape and painted it red. The man heaved the rock off to one side down the mountain and returned to where the woman was standing, hands fluttering, saying something to him and then looking nervously both ways up and down the trail. She needn't have worried. Apart from Wayne they were alone there and would be for quite a while. He had a good view of the trail and it was empty.

It seemed to be just dawning on her that they – that *she* – had actually just killed somebody. It was not just her hands – he could see even from up here that her whole body was shaking. He noted that it was a very good body. The tight jeans and T-shirt made that clear. He didn't know which was more attractive, the body or what he'd just watched it do.

The man seemed calmer. He wrapped his arms around her and held her for a moment.

Wayne could hear a muffled sobbing.

After a moment he let go and moved back to the dead man, took each of his wrists and started dragging. The head lolled sideways and left bloody skid-marks across the path. The dead man's expensive-looking running shoes scraped out their own trail.

And Wayne wondered how in hell they were expecting to get away with this.

It was going to be hard to clean up the mess down there. Head-wounds did a lot of bleeding. This one sure did. And even the most mentally deficient cop was probably going to check the slope above the place a corpse had landed.

He watched as the man dug a small hiker's backpack out of the brush beside the trail, turned the dead man over and slipped his arms through the shoulder straps, turned him again and hitched it together across his chest.

Hiking accident, thought Wayne.

Sure, maybe.

But there was still the problem of the bloody trail.

It was only when the body disappeared down off the rockface and he heard the long silence and then the dim, far-away splash that he realized that these people were smarter than he'd thought and maybe even knew what they were doing – that in fact they'd chosen the site pretty well. There was a stream down below that would be running deep and fast these days with all the rain they'd been having. He couldn't see it from where he was but he and Susan had passed it on the way up.

The body would carry.

Not bad, he thought. Not bad at all.

If they were lucky they might even get a little more rain tonight or tomorrow morning to wipe the slate clean altogether. He wondered if they'd checked the weather reports.

He bet they had.

He smiled. Watching them was absolutely the best damn time he'd had in years. Even now, as they were getting ready to leave. Even as the man kicked dirt across the path and pulled off his bloody shirt, turned it inside out and wet it from a thermos, used it to wipe the blood off his face and hands and stuffed it into a second, larger backpack he'd hidden with the smaller one in the brush; then took a clean shirt out of it and put it on.

The woman just sat there on a rock, watching, slack, as though her legs might not be up to supporting her. The man took a roll of plastic wrap out of the pack and wrapped the bat and put that in there too along with the thermos and zipped it shut. He slipped the pack over his shoulders and they were ready.

And the nicest thing happened then.

The man turned and looked up the mountain.

And Wayne knew him.

The man was a customer over at the Black Locust Tavern. Came in now and then.

A scotch drinker, he thought.

He didn't know his name.

He watched the woman rise – it seemed as though she was going to be able to walk on out of here after all – and the two of them move away down the path. Just a pair of hikers out for a walk on a nice sunny day. If somebody passed them and thought that the woman looked a little shaky – well, it was no easy climb.

The whole thing, Wayne thought, including the killing, had probably taken less than ten minutes.

Ten minutes to kill a guy. It was amazing.

He waited until they were out of sight, and then he started down.

There was blood splashed along the rocks where they'd killed him, droplets in the brush and a small pool staining the grass. He pulled this up with his hands. The blood was half-dried and sticky, the color of rust. The grass clung to the palms of his hands. He scattered it and dug up the dirt beneath until no trace was left and rubbed some more dirt into his hands.

They'd done a piss-poor job on the trail so he finished scuffing it up for them with his Reeboks and a sharply pointed stick. He rubbed some dirt along the rockface. There was nothing he could do about the splattered brush but he had made the whole scene less noticeable. You would have to be looking for something now. You would not just trip across it.

It took him a while to find the body.

In fact it was getting on to late afternoon when he finally saw it drifting back and forth in a gently whirling eddy between some granite boulders a

22

quarter mile or so from where they'd killed him.

He did not approach directly but waited until he was certain there was no one around either moving up or downstream or coming down the mountain from above. At this hour it was unlikely but he did not want to take any chances. He waited until he was confident that all he was hearing was rushing water and birds and forest-sounds and then he waded in.

The body floated face down. The pants, jacket and shirt were sodden and looked too big for him now. The backpack rode high, almost to his neck, and was skewed to the left. Wayne took hold of a clammy pale wrist and pulled him halfway up onto one of the rocks so that just his legs dangled in the water. The right leg had twisted in its socket during his fall. The knee pointed almost completely behind him now.

He examined the head-wound, washed partly clean but still red and glistening. It looked like a roast or a steak left to defrost too long in its clear plastic wrap on the counter, a deep rich spoiled red, lying in a pool of blood thinned and diluted by water.

He touched its rim, touched the strands of soft thick brain-matter the stream had urged free along the side of the wound, saw small sharp shards of bone poking through the way the broken shell of a clam will embed itself in its soft delicious mantle.

He touched the hard jagged edge of broken skull, thinly draped with silky flesh and coarse strands of muddy dark hair.

He picked a twig away.

He turned the body over. It was the eyes he wanted to see. The body was heavy with water and it was hard to move but he managed to get it over on one shoulder and pulled and finally the legs flopped over splashing in the water, followed by the torso and the head.

The eyes were not what he had expected.

He had expected shock. Maybe even wonder. Some romantic final gaze into the infinite. A look of startled wide-eyed amazement like they wrote about in all the books. Like you saw in the movies. The look of somebody who's seen deep into his own mortality. Then past it.

But the eyes were hardly open.

Just thin dull slits of grey filmed over. Like the guy was drunk, maybe, and sleeping off a hangover.

It was *boring*.

He turned the body over, let it slide back into the stream. He gave it a push with his foot so that it escaped the eddy, turned slowly into the current and began moving downstream. He watched it drift away. He had done the same with toy wooden boats once long ago.

He guessed that he had learned something.

It was the killing – not the death – that mattered.

23

It was not the product of the kill, which was nothing but meat and emptiness when you got down to it, though the person you killed wasn't there anymore and that was something. But the act itself, the moment of the taking and the losing.

That was classy. That was important.

He wondered what it felt like.

No dog, no cat. But a man.

Maybe one of these days he'd ask them.

It was getting dangerously close to dusk. The stream had turned metallic black. The sky was grey – as though they indeed might see more rain tonight. He decided he'd better get out of there.

It was a fact that people got lost on this mountain every year.

This time it was definitely going to be the other guy.

SUNDAY

Three

The morning after the murder she dreamed that she had shut both her cats up inadvertently in the oven. She had seen them crawl in there, had simply forgotten and turned the oven on and closed the oven door and left the kitchen.

It wasn't until she heard the yowling, the hideous hissing scratching sounds that she remembered and hurried in from her bedroom.

She opened it and there was Beastie covered with Vinni's blood, her black coat glistening, shaking Vinni by the neck, tearing wide the open gash from ear to shoulder with her two front paws and glaring out at Carole as though to say, *You did this. You made us crazy. You see what you did?* Vinni was dead, her poor head lolling, tongue longer than she had ever seen it in life protruding through bloody teeth.

She woke up crying, aching, to Sunday morning and the first thing she did was look past Lee's shoulder out the window.

It had rained overnight as they'd hoped.

The grass on her long sloping lawn was wet and green and there were puddles on the fieldstone porch.

She guessed that they were lucky.

She didn't feel lucky.

She felt frightened.

Lee was still sleeping, the sheet bunched up beneath him. She looked at the clock. The clock read eight-fifteen. Three-and-a-half hours' sleep. They'd both had more than their share to drink last night – more than they were used to. Adrenalin had run high in each of them until well into the morning. She supposed that fear would do that to you. The bed stunk of sweat and exhaustion.

She looked at him. He looked like a stranger. A stranger she'd known for a good two years now. She didn't want to wake him.

She needed some time alone before she could face anybody. Even him.

Maybe a lot of time.

She got up and pulled on a robe and walked to the kitchen. There was coffee in the pot left over from the night before. She poured some and put it in the microwave and set the timer for seventy seconds. The cats were circling her, brushing against her ankles, so she fed them, pulled the tab on the can of Friskies and spooned it out onto two plates and watched them attack in their accustomed spirit of happy near-starvation. She leaned back against the counter and watched them.

Beast was all black except for a paintbrush-stroke of white down along her bib. Vinni was a golden grey-and-white tabby. Howard had picked them both up for her at the ASPCA a year apart from one another. The nicest thing he'd ever done for her.

That was years ago. Beast was six and Vinni was five.

And there was the goddamn trembling again.

Last night it had seemed it would never go away – her whole body shaking, coming at her in spasms. A drink would fix it for a moment but last night even the drinking was strange. The scotch would wear off in no time, leaving her vividly sober and remembering what they'd done and right back where she started again. Shaking.

She'd been afraid of Howard when he was alive.

She was afraid of him now that he was dead.

What had changed?

She'd thought that once he was gone at least that sense of inhabiting these all-too-frequent moments of desperation would finally go away. That sense of *possession*. He'd created it after all. He'd put it there.

But it hadn't. Not at all.

It had woken up with her this morning.

It was here with her now making coffee.

You've got to give it time, that was what Lee said and he was probably right. But it was also all too possible that the only thing they'd managed to do here was to make a horrible situation immeasurably worse than they'd imagined.

What in God's name had they been thinking?

What had ever made them think they could kill a man and make things better?

Even someone as cruel and . . . *implacable* as Howard.

Even if they got away with it.

Which, for all their planning and precautions she couldn't help but feel was very much in doubt. There was Lieutenant Rule for one thing. Rule or someone like him. And her as-yet untested ability to make herself over into a world-class liar.

They were crazy.

The timer buzzed on the microwave.

She sipped the coffee. Either it was stale or her mouth was stale. Probably both. She carried it into the living room and sat on the sofa and

28

cradled the cup in her hands, feeling its warmth. The warmth helped stop the shaking.

She sat back and stared and drank the coffee until her mind went blank and empty – until it felt like there was nothing left at all inside her – just externals. Soft couch and warm cup and the morning birds on the lawn outside the window.

She wanted to shower alone, without Lee.

Somehow that was necessary.

It wasn't his fault. She didn't think it was.

He had only been reacting to her pain.

Though the idea to kill him – if you could even dignify it with the word idea, born as it was on a night of utter blinding rage after what, finally, Howard had seen fit to do to her – the actual *utterance* had been Lee's.

We've got to kill him. He'll never go away. You know that. He's got to die.

She had never disagreed. Not by then.

By then Howard had made her a believer.

But now she needed to grasp and hold the morning without Lee the same way she was holding this cup of coffee here, to be alone with the morning, to get used to the sheer cold fact of morning and listen to the familiar roar of the shower drowning out every other sound, feel it pound across her body as hot as possible and soap herself until she was cleaner than anyone would ever need or want to be, soap her body over and over just like she'd needed to yesterday but couldn't because first they had to stop at Jim Clarke's service station as soon as they got off the mountain to fill up the BMW and pass some time talking with Jim so that he'd remember them, then make their seven o'clock dinner reservation at Foxfire. They had to be seen in public as close to the time of Howard's death as possible. So that by the time she got to shower last night it had been nine. By then her anxiety had been so intense she could barely stand the spray on her nerve-ends, could barely stand to towel dry – or after that, the feel of the fine silk teddy against her skin.

Do it now, she thought. Before he wakes and wants company. Before he needs to talk again.

She dropped the robe off her shoulders to the marble bathroom floor and stood gazing at herself naked in the mirror.

Her flesh looked exactly the same to her.

It was amazing.

As though it and she had gone through nothing extraordinary whatsoever.

It would have been much more appropriate to find some new scarring there next to the old.

To find stigmata.

She reached down and turned on the water – *hot* – and stepped into the scorching spray.

'I'd suggest a movie,' he said.
 'What?'
 'Seriously. We've got to get our minds off this. Wait it out. Be patient. We're not going to hear anything today.' He hesitated. 'Not unless . . .'
 'Not unless they find him.'
 'That's right. And I don't think they will. Do you?'
 She shrugged. His question was meant to be rhetorical but it also had an edge to it.
 Reassure me.
 She'd showered and brushed her teeth until her gums were sore and the coffee still tasted foul and chalky.
 'Look,' he said. 'Tomorrow's what we've got to think about. When he doesn't show up at the office first thing Monday morning like they're used to. Sooner or later the police are going to get around to questioning us and it could be as early as, say, tomorrow afternoon. We've got to be up for that, Carole. Physically and mentally. So what are we supposed to do all day, keep drinking?'
 She stared at him blankly across the table. 'So you're suggesting a movie?'
 'Why not?'
 'You could concentrate on that?'
 He smiled a little. 'I suppose I could give it a shot.'
 'Jesus.'
 He didn't like the way this was going.
 She looked bad for one thing. It was the booze last night and the lack of sleep. She sounded alternately depressed and jumpy – to him at least, though he supposed his ear was more attuned to her than most would be. But if she was still acting this way tomorrow and the police did want to question her you never knew who might get to thinking what, and that was not good for their . . . situation here.
 He didn't know exactly what he'd expected of her. But he'd expected more strength. More firmness. More of an acceptance of what they'd done and why it had needed doing.
 More sense of relief.
 She didn't seem relieved.
 In fact there were times she looked like she'd lost her best friend.
 Which Howard sure as hell wasn't.
 He supposed it was too early for that. Relief would come later. When Howard was officially an accident and they were safe again.

Howard *would* be an accident.

He willed it.

He finished the coffee and stood, tightening the towel around his waist.

'I'm going to go get dressed,' he said. 'Think about it. If you come up with any better ideas I'd be happy to hear them. Honest.'

In the bathroom he went to the mirror and checked the damage. The eye was a little puffy but it wasn't going to go black on him, thank God. The lip was cut but not too badly, no worse than a cold and chapped lips could account for. The worst things didn't show. He'd taken a deep nasty bite out of the left side of his mouth where Howard had hit him and his left upper incisor and two front uppers were moveable inside the gum and they hurt like hell. He'd been popping aspirin since yesterday afternoon. He popped two now at the handcut marble sink.

Dammit. I don't like this, he thought.

What in hell got me into this?

Carole had of course. Who she was and where they'd arrived together.

That very strange place indeed.

The two of them. A pair of failed romantics wanting something back from lives that had each gone down the toilet long ago, wanting something they had missed for a very long time.

Trying to help each other get it.

That was what it was about, wasn't it?

Howard's murder?

He had yet to speak the word aloud.

He still suspected it was going to be worth it.

If they didn't get caught.

If she didn't shape up soon they could very well get caught.

He knew this much – the police always looked at the wife or husband first, and looked hard, if there was any question of homicide. He could only hope that either she'd rise to the occasion if and when it arose or that the police would assume Howard's death was a hiking accident the way they were supposed to in the first place and let the matter drop. Howard was a hiker, a skier, a rabbit hunter and a sailing enthusiast. Every one of them accident-prone activities to one degree or the other.

But what if they didn't?

Then Carole was going to have to carry the ball.

And somehow he had to get her ready for that.

He dropped the towel on the brass fourposter bed and went to the dresser for socks and underwear, to the closet for slacks and a shirt. Some of the shirts toward the back didn't belong to him. When Howard had left (been kicked out, actually – she'd simply changed the locks on him) it all had happened so fast that a lot of his clothes were still in here, months after the divorce. In fact Howard's things were everywhere, scattered throughout the house. It had been easy to find things, belongings of his, suitable for the backpack.

Once this was over it would all have to go.

He dressed. He felt calmer now.

Not like her.

The peak of his own anxiety had passed holding that goddamn bat over Howard's head after the second blow took him down, and he realized that they *had* to kill him now, there was no turning back, that they were in it every inch of the way. He'd hesitated, feeling all of a sudden weak as a kitten, shaky in the legs, the Louisville Slugger no longer the avenging jawbone of Samson's ox but a thousand-pound weight riding over him, and bearing down.

Thank God for Carole.

Howard was stronger than some soft businessman who owned an eighty-condo, eighty-four-room ski resort had any right to be. He'd damn near botched it.

And then where would they be?

In jail.

If there was one thing Howard had plenty of it was lawyers.

He slipped on the new pair of running shoes he'd bought a week ago for exactly this very occasion, for this morning, and laced them up. The old ones were ashes in the furnace along with the baseball bat and the rest of yesterday's clothes, both his own and Carole's. His first order of business today would be to clean that out thoroughly, bag the ashes and deposit them in Little River.

But then after that they had the whole long day ahead of them.

And another. And another.

He really hadn't been kidding about the movie.

They needed something to get their minds off things. Carole was in no shape to go visit somebody and neither was he to tell the truth, and this was no good place to just sit around all day. Sooner or later they were going to get on each other's nerves, they'd have trouble standing each other's company. Their *exclusive* company. A drive through the countryside was out of the question for the same reason.

No. They should just hit a movie. Sit in the dark for a couple of hours and let somebody else's daydreams or even their nightmares wash on over them. Have dinner at some restaurant and then come home to bed.

Sleep maybe.

And wait.

He hoped that when this was over they'd have a sex life again. They didn't now. They'd barely touched since Thursday. It was a first for them.

32

And it was perverse, really, because they needed to be closer than ever now. And along with simply having her – and having her around him all the time, to look at and be with and touch and, to be honest, having her lifestyle too and the freedom, cash and time to do whatever the hell they wanted to do together – he counted on the sex. He needed the sex.

It was part of what had got him here.

He knew that now. He hadn't at the time.

He wondered if he resented her for that. That hold on him.

It was disconcerting. Like being a kid again who couldn't handle the raging hormones. No one else had ever brought that out in him to such a degree or sustained it for so long. Not like Carole.

He walked past her sitting in the kitchen in front of the empty cup of coffee right where he'd left her and went down the stairs to the basement.

To bag what was left of Saturday.

He would deal with Carole later. He'd find some way to deal with her. Coach her, reassure her. He had to.

First things first.

Four

It was a slow night and Wayne noticed them the minute they walked in the restaurant.

From then on it was hard to pay attention to his customers. So that it was just as well there were only a few of them.

He felt almost as excited as he had back on the mountain. He was watching two people who had killed somebody go about their business as though nothing had happened, sitting not twenty-five feet away from him in their little alcove and ordering from the same menu as everybody else in there, as the old couple behind them and the family of four and the three yuppie banker types across the room.

Phenomenal!

It was just before nine when they arrived and Lacy, the new girl, was waiting their table, looking cute and trim in her regulation Trapp-family Alpine skirt, puff-sleeved blouse and suspenders. They ordered two drinks each – Bloody Marys for her and Dewars rocks for him. He thought that the woman looked a little haggard, a little strained, but she was dressed very nicely in a red silk blouse and dark-colored skirt, black or navy, with dangly silver earrings and silver bracelets on her wrists. Her hair was dark and long and shiny.

They ate silently, talking just occasionally.

What struck him so hard was that *you would never know*.

They looked just like everybody else in there. Ordinary people. Better-looking maybe than most couples but other than that . . .

He could barely keep his mind on Ensminger and Thompson drinking drafts in front of him enough to keep their glasses filled. They were talking about fifties music or some damn thing and tried to involve him now and then but what did he know about fifties music, and what did he care? He much preferred the trio of housewives down at the end of the bar who were nursing their drinks and bitching about their families. They'd leave him a lousy tip. But at least they were leaving him alone.

He took to polishing glasses, mindless activity, so he could watch them.

He saw nothing that would call the slightest attention to them. They were invisible.

34

He made himself an ice tea with lemon and sipped it through a straw.

By about twenty after ten they finished eating and were working on their coffee – and Wayne was starting to get nervous.

Dammit!

If there were only some way to get out from behind this bar then maybe he could follow them. Find out who they were and where they lived.

He had to stop himself from snapping at Ensminger when he ordered another beer. Not that the fucking idiot would notice anyway. He was already more than halfway in the bag. He hoped he wrapped his fucking Honda Civic around a goddamn tree.

He was a slave to this place!

None of the waitresses could cover for him. And none of the other bartenders were on tonight.

He was on his own.

It wasn't fair. To be this close. To the mystery. To knowing them.

To finding out what it felt like.

He knew by now that eventually he had to talk to them. His life, his happiness and sanity, depended upon it.

He'd thought of literally nothing else all night. There was something he needed from them. He didn't know what it was exactly but something. Poking and prodding its way into his sleep, into his daydreams. He met the feeling coming and going. It was everywhere.

Sure, probably there'd be other times. Other chances. They'd come in again or at least the man would, he had in the past and there was every reason to figure he would again. It could be weeks, though. Months!

He felt a tightness in his throat.

Something wanted saying.

Something wanted doing.

He shoved Ensminger's beer in front of him, took a five out of the man's change and went to the register, scooped a dollar and a half out of the cash drawer and slapped it down on the bar.

And then looked back to their table.

And smiled.

Because Lacy was standing in front of them. Polite and smiling, accepting the man's credit card. His Visa or his Mastercharge.

Which meant he didn't have to follow them.

Because the card would have a name. And the card would come to him. To the register.

The name that was on the card would be in the telephone book.

It had to be.

'Buy you one?' he said to Ensminger and Thompson.

They looked at him. Wayne was *buying*?

He knew that look. They were going into the book for that.
RETAL.
It didn't matter. He still felt expansive.
He considered that it wasn't going to hurt his tip any either.
He poured the beers even though Ensminger was only half-finished with the one he'd just served him and, grinning – *who the hell cared how he looked to them?* – waited for Lacy.

MONDAY

Five

Lieutenant Joseph Rule brushed some imaginary lint off his slacks and regarded his therapist from across the room. Marty as usual was getting right to the point.

Some days, he thought, I could deck you. You strike like a goddamn snake.

'What did she *say* to me?' he said.

Marty didn't look like a therapist. He was built like a small black angus bull actually and if Rule did decide to deck him he probably should get an upgrade on his medical insurance before he tried.

'She told me to go away, basically. Not to call so much, not to go out there for a while. That she needed to get on with her life.'

Marty raised his eyebrows and nodded. The eyebrows and the nod were a cinch to translate. *Well, she probably does, doesn't she?*

'I told her I understood. That I should probably get on with my life too.'

'You said that?'

'Yeah.'

'Did you mean it?'

He'd thought about that.

The first time he and Ann had separated three months ago he thought he'd go crazy. He could get through his workday all right but after that all he wanted to do was go home and drink. Which most nights is what he did.

He called her constantly, Vermont to California, every night while he was only on his second or third vodka and still sober enough to make some sense. He guessed she'd heard his pain and maybe still had some hopes for the two of them, that he still might eventually work out his problem, his unwillingness to commit to her and her daughter Chrissie full-time – and finally, last month, she'd suggested he come out again and visit.

He had some vacation time coming.

He'd jumped at the chance.

It was some vacation.

It was all of two days before everything surfaced again.

'Yeah, I think I did mean it. I think it finally got through to me, the kind of hell I was putting her through, six years of me coming and going all the time, Here two days and gone five, here three days and gone four. She went all the way to California to get away from that. She said things to me like, Chrissie and I are always saying to each other, when Joe comes out we'll do this, we'll do that. We'll go to Disneyland. Always putting things off because they *like* doing things with me but the point is they're *not doing them.* Because I'm not there. I'm here.'

'Yes, but I don't get it. What's that got to do with you getting on with your own life?'

'Maybe I just saw her point this time. I'm not going to change. I'm just stopping *them* from changing. When they probably need to. I think I just accepted the inevitable. Who I am. What I am. I'm fucked. That's all.'

'You're not fucked.'

'Oh no? Then what am I doing sitting here paying you seventy bucks an hour?'

'You're paying me so you don't *get* fucked.'

'By whom?'

'By you. Joe Rule.'

Marty shifted in his plush black leather chair, starting to get up, the signal that their hour was over. There was a clock on the wall directly over Rule's head and he'd often tried to catch the man's eyes going up there but he never had. He thought there was something sort of talented about that.

'Hey, we finally got through one. A whole session. How about that.'

The beeper went off in his jacket pocket.

He flicked it off and laughed.

'Almost.'

Marty shrugged. 'The only thing left to do is to hand me the check. We got through it.'

Rule fished the check out of his wallet. 'Here. Toward that place at the Vineyard.'

'I already have a place at the Vineyard.'

'You don't just rent anymore?'

'Not since last year.'

'Hell. Some cop. I don't know shit about you.'

'You're not supposed to.'

'Mind if I use the phone?'

'Do I ever?'

Rule dialed in. He got Rita on the desk and then Covitski.

'What's up?'

'Where are you?'

'Never mind where I am. What's up?'

'Okay, fine. Be a pain in the ass. You've been leaning on a guy named Harold Gardner. Keeps fucking around on a restraining order. You and the ex have been in touch a few times, am I right?'

'Right.'

'Well, see, if I knew where you were I might ask you to go on over there and have a little conversation with her. I mean if you're not out in Jersey or Connecticut or something. You know, if you're close by. I don't want this to be inconvenient for you, you know?'

'Enough, Covitski. What's the problem?'

'Secretary over at the, what is it . . . Inn at Green Gables, resort he owns, says he didn't show up for work today and didn't call in. Says this is very unusual for the gentleman. She's been trying his condo and his car phone all day. Nothing. So I figured . . .'

'You figured you could hit me with this sack of shit while you go out for lunch. Why's anybody bothering with this, anyway? How long's he been missing – four hours? Christ, I know the guy. He's rich and spoiled and he'll fuck anything that doesn't walk on all fours. Forget the wife. Check his cocktail waitresses. Hold on a minute.'

He turned to Marty. Cupped his hand over the mouthpiece. 'Is somebody waiting outside?'

Marty was sitting again. He'd lit up a Marlboro. Rule liked that about the man. He never smoked during sessions but he did before and after. You smelled it when you walked into the room. If you minded the smoke you got yourself another therapist. Simple as that.

Marty nodded. 'Yes. Take your time, though.'

He knew that was bullshit. For Marty more than most people time was definitely money.

'All right,' Rule said into the phone. 'I'll go out there. But I'm putting this on your tab, understand me?'

'Sure, Joe.'

He hung up the phone.

'Thanks, Marty. I'll call you when I know what the rest of the week looks like, okay?'

'Fine.' He got up and opened the door. 'How's the dolls' house coming?'

In his spare time, such as it was, Rule was building Chrissie a dolls' house, working out in his garage. He had been for over a year now, since long before the two of them had left Vermont. He saw no reason to stop now that he and Ann were quits. It hadn't been Chrissie's idea.

Though how in hell he was going to pack it up eventually and ship it out to her was a little beyond him. The damn thing weighed a ton.

'Exterior's finished. I'm papering the walls and laying in the molding.'

In fact his work on the house was two bedrooms and a second-floor hallway from completion. For some reason he didn't feel like telling Marty that.

'I'll call you,' he said.

The drive to Barstow was normally only ten minutes straight up 100 North. But they finally had a warm clear day so there were summer tourists out doing what tourists did, antiquing, admiring the scenery, heading for the resorts along Mount Haggerty. License plates from New York, Florida, and Massachusetts dawdled up ahead of him. It was nothing like ski season or even the fall leaves-season but it slowed him down a little.

He had time to admire the mountain the Abnaki Indians had called Mose-de-be-Wadso – Head Like a Moose – braced with cumulus clouds. Rule had never really seen the moose there. He didn't figure he was missing anything. He thought that a moose ranked right up with the anteater as one of the ugliest animals that ever lived and that the mountain was much prettier than that.

He went straight through the blinking light at the center of town, turned right at Snow's grocery and began to climb.

The road didn't look like much at first but that was deceptive. If you lived up here you were talking a quarter million in property minimum, even with the economy kicking hell out of housing. As you climbed the homes got bigger, the parcels of land more extensive. The Gardner place was about three-quarters of the way up. Which meant that Carole Gardner was looking at about two-and-a-half million and change in real estate alone.

Rule didn't ordinarily sympathize much with somebody worth that kind of money but in the case of Carole Gardner he'd already made an exception.

The woman had married the Real Estate Mogul from Hell.

There was no other way to put it. The man was arrogant, drunk, and abusive. Into knives and guns and kinky sex. Often, together.

Howard Gardner considered himself an aristocrat.

Rule recalled him vividly. He'd had the pleasure of serving him a restraining order – then later of prying him off her lawn, loaded, early one morning. Then still later, of arresting him.

From what he'd learned – not just from Howard's wife but from people who knew them both – the marriage had existed largely as a reign of terror. Carole was Howard's partner, half-owner of the resort and supposedly very strong on the financial side while Howard rode herd over his staff and did the political and social schmoozing.

He supposed they must have been a pretty good team for a while. One day they turned around and they were rich.

She bought the big house on Stirrup Iron Road. Howard started drinking and fucking around like his idol was Teddy Kennedy.

She complained to him about it. Once.

He put her in the hospital with a broken rib.

That was the beginning.

Rule didn't fully understand the battered-wife syndrome but he knew it when he saw it. When Carole first got up the nerve to talk to somebody in the department about Howard she talked first to Officer Joyce Clarke and then she talked to Rule. And that was what he saw. A successful, intelligent woman so demoralized she could barely speak to them above a whisper. They both advised her to press charges. Advised it strongly.

She said she'd consider it.

She went home.

That night he tied her face-down to the bed, raped her, and went at her with belt and belt-buckle until her back, legs and butt were so bloody she threw out the sheets in the morning. He passed out drunk on top of her. In the morning he untied her and went to work.

While Howard was working she was busy too.

Something about this last one, something about him lying there on top of her, lying in her blood all night, had finally gotten to her.

She changed the locks, filed for a restraining order and got herself a lawyer.

Rule remembered serving the order.

Gardner was sitting at the bar over at Hunger Mountain talking to George Hammond and Bob Walker, two brand-new Barstow city councilmen, telling them a story about a blind bankrobber over in West Guilford who had pulled his stickup and then asked the teller to please walk him to the door, he was nervous and he was blind, he couldn't remember exactly where the door was. The teller refused and phoned the police while the guy walked around bumping into walls trying to find his way out of there.

Rule knew the story. He even knew the arresting officer. Gardner and the councilmen thought it was a pretty funny story and so did he. Only now with Howard telling it, it also struck him as cruel.

You know the one about the real-estate developer who thinks he's a prize stud? he said.

Gardner looked like he'd swallowed something still alive and twitching. No, he said. What.

He got gelded in the courts, said Rule. And handed him the order.

It should have ended with that but it didn't.

Gardner after the divorce was as bad as Gardner before the divorce. Worse.

He'd bought her out of Green Gables as part of the settlement and she'd taken up with a man named Lee Edwards, Howard's one-time manager over at the Inn and then, since meeting her, manager at Woodchip Pines.

A step down but what the hell. She had plenty for both of them.

The problem was that Howard wasn't leaving her alone. He acted like he fully expected her back, Edwards or no Edwards.

He'd even held onto a quarter-million-dollar insurance policy in her name.

Rule thought the guy was crazy.

He thought that with an ego that big Howard could probably be president someday.

He pulled into the circular driveway and cut the motor. His old Chrysler wagon coughed once and then obeyed. He sat in silence for a moment, her white BMW parked in front of him like somebody's snooty cousin.

The house stood on a green well-tended ridge with about three acres of woodland rolling down the hill behind it. He'd been inside a couple of times. The interior was light and elegant if a little too modern for his tastes and a lot too sprawling. Four bedrooms, two floors. Long and wide. Imported Italian marble sinks with slim gold faucets in the bathrooms. Restaurant-sized refrigerator in the kitchen. A circular bed and massive new four-posters of brass and mahogany. Sauna and Jacuzzi.

He remembered pulling Howard off the lawn one winter night at four in the morning, the man's voice carrying for blocks through the clear crisp air and empty streets. He was calling her a whore one minute and telling her she'd come crawling back to him the next. Waving a litre bottle of Glenlivet with about an inch left in the bottom.

'Come on, Howard,' Rule had said and took him by the arm. It was an unexpectedly muscular arm beneath the rumpled hand-tailored jacket.

'She loves it,' he grinned. 'She called you? She called the cops? Hey, that's just a game she plays.'

'Sure,' Rule said and cuffed him.

Howard looked surprised. Then he nodded.

'You know what?' he said. 'You're very efficient. I like you. You wanna job?'

He remembered her standing at the door, a beautiful woman, haggard and worn. Edwards standing behind her, holding onto her shoulders as though he was afraid she might break.

She didn't break. But that wasn't the end of it either.

He went through Howard's file in his head.

He'd harassed them by phone every night for two months running, calling at all hours of the morning. Threats. Obscenities. The usual. Except that Howard really had a flair for it. *I'm going to carve you slit to slit*, he told her, *from cunt to lips. Then I'm going to pull you open and fuck your liver.*

What a guy.

44

She changed her number. Twice. Both times Howard found it. Finally they put a tracer on her phone. The calls stopped dead. They removed it after two weeks and they started up again. Rule didn't know how he knew, but he did.

He paid a fine for drunk and disorderly and for violation of a restraining order for the episode out on the lawn and that was the last the court system ever saw of him.

Not Rule, though.

In mid-March he got a call saying Carole Gardner was at the station filing a complaint against her ex-husband and would he please come by. He found her in Joyce's office. She was nearly hysterical.

Around noon that day Howard had climbed through an open window off the patio. When she came out of the laundry room he put a Colt revolver to her head and moved her onto the couch, where he raped her, punched her, wrapped the cord of a standing lamp around her neck and toyed for a while with the notion of strangulation.

She said she'd come straight there to the station because she was afraid that if Edwards came home from work and she had to tell him about it Edwards might be mad enough to kill him. Howard was not the only one who owned a handgun. There was a .357 magnum in her top dresser drawer.

Rule drove to Howard's office complex with an arrest warrant burning holes in his pocket. Howard was sitting at his desk with Bill Clayton and Harold McDermott, two of the stockholders in Gables, Inc., his company. The stockholders swore that Howard had been with them all day long on a drive to Wolfeboro, New Hampshire for a look at the Mountolive Inn for possible purchase by their corporation and they were both perfectly willing to sign affidavits to that effect.

Both men were unshakable and maddeningly smug. Like rape was just fine by them if it happened to be your ex-wife you were raping.

The fact that both these guys were divorced themselves was not lost on him.

But he had no case.

Then finally just last month he had another call from her. It was puzzling.

She'd sounded extremely upset again, he could barely understand what she was saying. He'd tried to calm her, but then he'd had to put her on hold for a moment while Hamsun, his chief, ran over some detail on the arrest report of a suspect in the breaking-and-entering item that had come in the night before.

By the time he got back to her all she would say was that she was sorry she'd bothered him, it was really nothing – and when he pressed her, said she was just afraid that Howard was *going* to do something, not that anything had actually *happened*, she was just afraid that something might. She sounded a little better by then so he'd had to let it go at that. He could hear Edwards in the background saying something to her but he couldn't make out what.

And that was the last he'd heard from her.

He walked up the fieldstone steps to the porch and rang the bell. He waited.

When she came to the door his first impression was that here it was nearly five o'clock and she looked like she'd just gotten herself ready and put together for the day. Her blouse and jeans looked crisp, like she'd just put them on. Her hair looked freshly brushed, makeup newly applied.

Rich people, he thought. She's probably changed clothes six times already.

She smiled and opened the door. He decided she looked a little tired but otherwise okay.

'Lieutenant Rule. Joe. Come on in.'

This is bullshit, he thought. Howard's been missing maybe eight, nine hours. There's nothing wrong here.

He watched her move through the hall ahead of him into the living room. The room was neat and tidy.

'What can I do for you? I just made coffee. Want some?'

She turned. The smile looked fine too, as far as he could see.

'No thanks. I don't want to hold you up. I was just wondering what you'd heard from Howard lately.'

She sighed and sat down on the couch. Rule joined her.

'Nothing, thank God.'

'Nothing? No phone calls?'

She shook her head. 'I think he's finally given up on me. Can you believe it? I thought he never would.'

'I was beginning to agree with you. Congratulations. When's the last you heard from him?'

She thought about it.

'I guess that would be . . . the night I phoned you. The middle of last month.'

'Nothing since?'

'Nothing. No.'

'I'd been wanting to ask you for a while, what was that all about? You sounded pretty bad there.'

She shrugged and shook her head again.

'Just another phone call. But this one was . . . worse than most.'

'How so?'

46

'Threatening. You know. He's going to do this to me and he's going to do that. I don't remember exactly what he said. Maybe I've blocked it. Or maybe it's just faded away into . . . into all the rest of them. Anyway, it upset me. So I phoned you. And then I thought, my God, it's just a telephone call, for Godsakes. You've had plenty. You ought to be used to them by now.'

She studied him a moment.

'Is this just a follow-up, Joe?'

'Not exactly. Your husband's – Howard's – secretary called. He didn't show up for work today. She can't seem to reach him.'

'So?'

Which was his reaction entirely.

He sighed. 'You know how it is. Howard's rich and he's connected. If he's missing, he gets missed. If it was the guy who mows his lawn nobody'd think twice about it. As it is, people worry.'

She looked at him again and he could see the implications of the thing slowly dawn on her. But all he read was normal curiosity.

'You're treating this as a potential homicide, aren't you?' she said.

'No. Not really. Not at this point. Right now it's just a missing persons. Is Lee still working over at the Pines?'

'Yes.'

'Could he have heard from Howard?'

'I think he would have said something.'

'Probably. Can you think of anywhere Howard might have disappeared to for a day or so?'

'God. Anywhere. He's got a sailboat docked over in Waterbury. There's a sister in Lexington, Massachusetts – June Rusch is her name. And he travels a lot scouting real estate. But I'd think his secretary would know about anything like that, wouldn't you?'

'I'd think so. Yeah.'

'Maybe he's got a girlfriend. Maybe that's why I haven't heard from him lately. Is that possible?'

'Sure it's possible. Got any candidates?'

She laughed. 'Anybody who works for him, is under thirty and dumb enough to find him charming. And I mean dumb – not stupid. Believe me, I know the difference.'

He smiled and got out of his chair. 'When Lee gets in have him give me a call, will you? Just in case he's heard from him. And if you think of anything – or anybody – let me know, okay?'

'I will.'

She walked him to the door. 'Do you think he could have . . . what do they call it? Bottomed out?'

He looked at her.

'The alcohol,' she said.

'It happens.'

'In that case he could be anywhere, couldn't he? Some bar somewhere. Some alley.'

He smiled. She didn't seem terribly unhappy about the prospect. But then he could see why either notion – a serious girlfriend or some final crashing bender – would agree with her. In either case she benefited. She'd be rid of the guy for a while.

'Not too many dark alleys in Barstow these days,' he said.

She flushed. 'It doesn't have to be Barstow, does it?'

'No, it doesn't. In fact with a man in Howard's position it's probably unlikely. Too many ways to embarrass yourself here. He'd probably head out of town if he had any clue he was about to go under. Anyway, thanks. I'll be in touch with you.'

'Okay,' she said. 'Good luck.'

As she opened the door he saw a tremble dart through her hand, coming and going like the passage of a sparrow in sudden flight. He headed down the stairs.

Nah, he thought. Couldn't be.

Around cops people got nervous.

And then he thought, sure it could.

There was the insurance money for one thing. He wondered if Howard still carried the policy. He'd have to check that.

He liked the woman. He didn't like to think about her that way but he had to.

It always could.

Six

'He was here already? Jesus.'

'He wants you to call.'

'Why?'

'In case you'd heard from Howard lately and didn't want to tell me.'

He was standing in the hallway at a distance from her. As though he were afraid of her. As though Rule might have contaminated her somehow. Not that she was looking for hugs and kisses now anyway.

What she wanted was another vodka.

She headed for the sideboard.

'You're drinking too much,' he said.

She dropped some ice into her glass.

'Talk to him first. Then decide how much is too much. For you. Not for me.'

'He was rough on you?'

'Not at all. He said it was just a missing persons, that the only reason he was talking to me is that we might have had some phone calls recently. That we might have heard from him.'

'How did you . . .?'

She whirled.

'I did just *fine*, Lee. I surprised myself. I'm probably the best little liar in Barstow right now, okay? Are you happy?'

He watched her pour the Stoli. She was gripping the bottle like the bottle had legs and just might run away from her. She thunked it down.

'For God's sake make your call,' she said. 'Believe me, you have nothing to worry about. He's not going to cross-examine you. Not today, anyhow.'

'Carole . . .'

His tone brought her up short. She knew what she'd been doing. In the hour since Rule left it was as though she'd spun a large protective cocoon all around herself, so that whatever she touched never really touched her back – not the couch nor the bottle nor even the warm summer air flowing around her – and that was the way she wanted it, the way she *needed* it to be.

But what had grown up inside the cocoon was ugly.

She put down the glass and walked over. Put her arms around him.

'I'm sorry.'

He hugged her.

'It's all right. We never expected this to be a breeze, did we?'

'No. We didn't.'

'I'll call him.' He pointed to the bottle. 'But I think I'd like one of those first. What the hell. I'm a hypocrite. Sue me.'

He kissed her. It was their first real kiss in days.

And even now she needed to break the embrace. She knew he could feel it. He let her go.

'Pour me one, will you?' he said. 'I want to go clean up. Then I want you to tell me everything you said to him. The whole conversation. Then I'll call.'

She nodded.

He leaned over and kissed her again. 'We're going to beat this, all right? We're not gonna pay for what that son of a bitch did to you.'

She smiled. Not much of a smile but the first, she realized, since he'd walked through the door. For a moment it was almost possible to believe him.

The red '93 Volvo was his prize possession. He'd bought it outright, in cash, as a present to himself after his mother was gone. Wayne sat behind the wheel gazing at the big house on the hill and thought that the Volvo fit right in with the neighborhood. Screw BMWs.

He was taking a risk but it was worth it.

The risk was that he'd been arrested just a month ago Saturday night driving home from a bar out on Stagecoach Road in Morrisville. They got him out of the car and had him walk straight ahead heel-to-toe and then close his eyes and stretch out his arms and touch his nose and then recite the alphabet and he was so damn furious and upset at being pulled over in the first place that he *forgot the fucking alphabet*! He did! He forgot it! He got to the letter P and skipped over *Q-R-S-T-U* and went directly to *V-W-X-Y-Z*.

He did it *twice*!

So they handcuffed him and shoved him in the squad car and he rode there silently, burning. At the station he blew .165 on the Intoxilyzer. Which was kind of high. They took his watch, his license, his cigarettes, his wallet and his belt and put him in a cinderblock holding cell painted white, the underpaint showing through like veins in a bloodshot eye.

There were six other guys in there, two of them real hardcases, you could see that right away. They were already dressed in jailhouse orange. They'd come up from the cells below. They were in for skipping bail on charges of armed robbery and they were big guys, pacing around, right in there with him! and four other guys who, like him, had done nothing but get themselves arrested on a lousy DWI.

They kept him there all night, sick, cold and hungry, with not even a clock or a wristwatch so you could know how long it was till daylight, most of that time in the same little cell with nothing but two rows of wooden benches and a shiny metal toilet sitting right in the middle of the goddamn room. He was glad he didn't have to take a leak or a shit, not with all those other guys looking on, not with those hardcases.

One of the drunks was crazy. He kept rolling back and forth on the bench saying, '*Cell!* You're in it now!' and laughing, and all Wayne wanted to do was kick him to death and curl up against the hard cold wall and disappear.

And later, get even.

There were notes in his book on arresting officer Gustafson, the crazy drunk, the two thugs in the cell, the judge – who was fat and female no less – the prosecutor named Barker and his own lawyer, who cost him nearly a grand, who joked with the prosecutor like they were old golfing buddies which probably they were, while Wayne listened to himself sentenced to six months' probation, maintenance fee forty bucks per month and conditional on a seven-week drinking-and-driving program which met every Saturday for Chrissake, his fucking *day off*, and which cost him *another* $200, plus the fine of $468. It was going to be easily two thousand dollars and a lot of wasted time before he was through.

So he had a lot of notes.

He was taking a risk but he couldn't imagine being unlucky enough to get caught driving without his license just this once. And there was simply no way he could resist coming up here for a look.

How could he?

Besides, he had to know the place, see how many people were living here, whether they had kids or dogs or anything. That kind of thing.

He saw no evidence of children. Just two cars in the wide circular driveway.

And no dogs.

It was just the two of them.

They were all alone.

He lit a cigarette and sat back to watch a while. The sun would be setting soon and he'd want to get out of there before it did. No sense acting suspicious. And he had to work tonight anyhow.

He saw the woman move past the bay window.
He thought, *They're absolutely all alone in this.*
They thought so, anyway.

TUESDAY

Seven

The man's hands were blue and white, the fingers like fat grey sausages floating bobbing in the shallow water, and Billy Whitsin could see the leg lying along the smooth-pebble bank twisted under him, the foot turned straight up into the air at an angle that was impossible unless you were a rag doll or made of pipecleaners like the stick-men little kids made in school or something, and somehow his head was wrong. Shaped wrong.

It was hard to see the head. It was lying in a pool of muddy water and there were crayfish after it, seven or eight crayfish – smooth brown armored backs glinting in the early morning sun. Billy had never seen so many in one place at one time. Big guys.

It was pretty amazing.

One thing he *could* see was that there were no eyes. In one of the places where an eye ought to be a long thin stringy almost transparent thing waved in the water like a strand of mucus.

Billy was a pretty good observer. Plus he was a very good citizen. He hadn't made Eagle Scout for nothing. Even though his mother kept expressing the concern that they were turning him into a little Nazi. He wasn't some little Nazi. He just respected order. His dad knew that. His dad was supportive. His dad had given him this two-pronged frog-spear he had here and a .22 rifle for his thirteenth birthday. He was a good observer and a good citizen and he knew enough to look closely so he could describe what he was seeing to the police but not to touch a thing, because they'd want to see it exactly as he'd found it.

He crouched down close to the man.

The stink didn't bother him. He had smelled dead things before and they all smelled the same.

Unless you had a skunk.

The man's blue nylon backpack was off one shoulder dangling into slightly faster-running water but the chest-strap had wound itself around his neck, the pack wasn't going anywhere. He had on muddy white Reeboks, dark blue or possibly black slacks, dark blue jacket and a checked blue-and-white shirt that was straining at the buttons because the man was so bloated. He could see a pasty slit of bellyflesh. The man's fly was

55

open, the zipper three-quarters down.

He wondered if there were crayfish in there too. Or up his pants legs.

He wouldn't be surprised.

It was too bad he couldn't really see the face so he could describe the man's features to the authorities because he knew they'd want to know that, but short of lifting the head up out of the muddy water there was nothing he could do about it.

He knew he was not supposed to touch the head or any other part of him so he didn't. Period.

The man was white, *caucasian*, and his hair was dark. That much he could tell them.

That, and that he had no eyes.

He carefully noted his exact location – the big rock downstream in the middle, the grouping of tall pines to the left and the thin leaning birches to the right. The water ran narrow here and fast.

He put down the frog-spear and took out his compass. The man's sausage-case right-hand index finger pointed due east across the stream. If he walked west for about a mile he'd come out to River Road. It was the fastest, most efficient way.

He dug his scout knife out of his pocket, picked up his frog-spear and started blazing trees.

He had done it dozens of times.

Nothing to it.

Halfway through the woods he found himself humming the theme from *Teenage Mutant Ninja Turtles*. March-step. Pacing himself. Humming the tune in short staccato bursts. He also found himself smiling. He hadn't thought about that dumb show or that song in a long time.

Not since he was a kid.

He cut deep into the flesh of a white birch tree and moved on.

Eight

Wayne dreamed of carnage.

In his dream he had crested a hill and looked down over a bare scorched plain. Fires still burned in the distance. Everywhere he looked across the vast open space he saw looting, death and dying.

An army of the dead come back to take the living. He saw men hacked to pieces with axes, stabbed with knives, executed by hanging, crucifixion, beheading. Trapped in nets and drowned in a filthy churning lake. Nailed through their skulls to blasted trees.

The army of the dead was huge, outnumbering the living by a thousand to one, driving them in panic like herd animals. The living trampled one another underfoot. Resistance was useless, escape impossible. A dying rich man waved feebly toward the walking corpse that was pillaging his life's fortune. The dead were everywhere. Hacking at throats with old rusty knives, hauling bodies, stacking them like cordwood in huge piles. He watched a squalling infant in the arms of its long-dead mother being eaten by a skeletal starving dog.

And woke.

The sheets were grey and damp.

Outside the window, the sun was high.

The dream lingered fresh and vivid in his mind. He held it there, galvanized, took it to the bathroom with him, savored it in the shower and on the pot and brushing his teeth.

Today, he thought.

No fucking around.

The dead lay siege to a tall tower filled with wailing women, calling for help, arms flailing. They hadn't a prayer.

Below them all the dogs were starving.

Nine

Rule sat hunched at his desk. For the moment the station was quiet.
Hamsun was in his office and Covitski was on the phone two desks down
and Warner and Tobias were booking some kid across the room. Apart
from them he was alone. There was a house on fire over on Sky Hill
Road and most of the uniforms were assisting with traffic and crowd
control.

He had Marty on the line. Not his machine for a change.

'You're calling from the station?'

'Yeah.'

'God, Joe. I feel honored.'

'Don't.'

It was true enough, though. Normally he'd have used a pay phone or else
called after work from home.

Marty was a secret. And Rule needed to keep him one. The only time that
most cops saw a shrink was when they'd shot somebody or somebody'd
shot a partner. Then it was mandated by the department. And even in that
case you went grudgingly and got the hell out as soon as possible. So his
colleagues would not understand. It was unthinkable to most of them that
a guy could feel the need to *talk* to somebody at seventy an hour. And talk
mostly about a woman, no less.

He couldn't blame them.

Naturally there were times when he talked about the job too.

And they wouldn't have understood that either.

The department was a closed shop. What happened stayed here. You
were not supposed to go around hiring scab labor.

'How's Thursday?'

'Thursday I've got a three o'clock and a six-thirty.'

'Say three.'

'And you'll call me if anything changes.'

'Marty, I always call you. You always say that and I always call you.
Get the hell off my case.'

'You don't mean that.'

'Marty, don't mess with me.' He glanced around. 'You know what?' he said. 'I dreamed about her. It doesn't happen much.'

'Last night?'

'Yeah.'

'And?'

'I don't remember a whole lot.'

'What do you remember?'

'She was lying in bed. She was asleep. I didn't want to wake her. I tiptoed away.'

'Tiptoed? You?'

'That's right.'

'Like a . . .'

'That's right, Marty. Like a thief in the night.'

Rule was glad he was finding this amusing.

'Hard to picture.'

'I managed.'

'You're not a thief, though. Are you?'

'Depends on your point of view.'

'I suppose. So maybe you're not over her.'

'Why?'

'The guilt. Sounds like guilt in the dream. You tiptoeing around like that. You put it behind you, you put it away, and the guilt generally disappears.'

'It does?'

'Generally.'

'Thursday at three, Marty.'

'Call me if anything comes up.'

He had a call on line two.

'Rule.'

It was Hamsun. *Guy's in a cubicle not twenty feet away* – Rule could see him through the glass – *but rather than move his fat eight-months-to-retirement butt off his chair he phones him.*

'Whatever you're doing, drop it. I want you to head out to River Road, junction of Maple, a little beyond that. Looks like we found your boy.'

'What boy?'

Hamsun sighed. Like Rule's the village idiot. Like he should simply intuit this.

Like he's not working five different cases simultaneously.

'Howard Gardner. Turns out he's a floater. Kid found him face-up about a mile through the woods out there.'

'It's not my case, George. I did Covitski a favor.'

'So keep on doing it. You and the wife are pals. Right?'

He sighed. 'East or west?'

'Huh?'

'East or west through the woods? East runs down through the Notch.'

'Uh . . . I dunno. East maybe. I'm not sure. Find out when you get there, right?'

'Yeah.'

He scratched *Marty – 3:00* on his desk calendar for Thursday, stuffed a notepad into his jacket pocket and went out to the car.

He wondered if Marty was right. He wondered if he had really given up on Ann or if he only thought he'd given up.

He wondered who was going to break the good news to Carole Gardner.

Or if she and Edwards knew already.

Howard. A floater. Who'd have thought it?

He guessed that anything was possible.

Ten

Ed Mason was a very nice man, Carole decided, with what appeared to be an only slightly unrealistic head for business from the look of his books. And he seemed open to suggestion. So there was room for her to teach him better work habits. If investing in his ten-room bed and breakfast was not going to make her rich exactly it looked like it would at least prove to be a pleasant and moderately profitable association.

Her BMW took the hill as effortlessly as usual. Old Mr Hennaker was out in front of his white, black-shuttered house watering the lawn. He saw the car and waved to her and she waved back.

Everything normal here.

See?

I haven't killed anybody at all yet today. How about that?

She could feel the stirrings of a headache.

Seeing Mason and doing business had been good for her. She had toured the dining room and bar with him, both rooms furnished with quality American country primitive antiques. The same was true of the sitting room with its big stone fireplace and the foyer. Then upstairs to the rooms. The rooms were a little too Laura Ashley for her tastes but there was a simplicity about them and a charm.

They talked about the renovation project and expansion of the restaurant and bar. As it stood, room rentals and his bar-and-restaurant business were bringing in about equal amounts of money. He could double his food and bar trade with no trouble at all. He had cornered one of the best chefs in Barstow. They were turning people away every night.

She'd gone over his books and her own involvement was definitely feasible.

It did her good to put her mind to something.

She'd forgotten about Howard for a while. Normal life had actually proved pleasant and exciting.

And now she was coming home again. There was the urge to turn right around. And go . . . *where*?

She saw the red Volvo parked in front of the Nichols' house. It struck her as a little unusual because the Nichols' car, a gorgeous new cobalt-blue

Infiniti J30, was not in the driveway.

Guests, she thought.

She pulled into the drive and cut the motor.

'Ms Gardner?'

He came out of nowhere.

The man was walking toward the car, taking his time, strolling down the driveway.

Where had he been? And where had he come from?

The hedges?

Looking for the gas meter?

The meter was in the house. They were all inside up here.

He carried a clipboard. He had a pencil in his hand and he was smiling. He was slim and neatly dressed in light brown baggy slacks, a cotton shirt and dark suede loafers.

'Yes?'

He extended his hand. 'Wayne Lock, Ms Gardner.' She shook it. The hand was wet and clammy. The man consulted his clipboard.

'This won't take but a minute. I've just got a few questions for you . . .'

'Excuse me. You're with whom?'

The man smiled and looked around. As if she'd just made some sort of joke. He tucked the pencil behind his ear.

'I'm with myself, Ms Gardner,' he said. 'That's obvious, right? I'm all by myself here.'

He reached around into his back pocket.

And suddenly there was a gun there.

A small black automatic in his hand. No cylinder like the magnum had. She could smell it now, oil and metal.

Pointed at her beneath the clipboard.

It was the smell that jolted her into flat reality. Without the smell she would not have believed it possible. Just a toy gun on a bright sunny day.

'I'm alone,' he said. *'Just like you.'*

The smile winked off and on again. Like he couldn't decide whether he needed it there or not.

'Please. What do you . . .?'

Just like that. She was already begging.

Please.

'What do I want? Like I said, I've got questions for you.' His eyes skittered left and right. 'Listen, I think we ought to go inside. That's a good idea, don't you think? Come on, let's the two of us go inside.'

Where was Lee?

Why was she alone here?

How could she go inside with him?

'I don't . . .'

'I'm not asking, Ms Gardner. I'm saying I think we ought to go inside. You understand me, right?'

The man's face was blank, unreadable.

He held the gun steady.

Her keys were in her hand, damp with sweat so that now she could smell them too. Metal again. Digging into the palm of her hand. She'd forgotten all about them.

She turned toward the door, turned her back to him. She didn't want to do that because she kept seeing the gun behind her but she knew she had no choice. The key wouldn't fit in the keyhole. Could she possibly have the wrong key here? No, of course not. The key slid in. She pushed the door open and looked at him.

'Ladies first,' he said.

And she couldn't really seem to bring herself to do that. The man was asking too much. She couldn't seem to step across the door jamb as though he were just anybody and she was just taking him on inside, an invited guest.

'I have no intention of harming you, if that's what you're afraid of. I mean, I'm not some rapist pervert or something. I want to be friends. Talk a little. Go on. Honest, I don't bite.'

'You . . . you have a gun.'

He laughed. 'That's because you don't know me yet. And I don't think you're exactly the type of person who lets complete strangers into her house every day. Am I right? So this way you'll talk to me. We can get rid of the gun once you know me a little better. Go ahead.'

She wasn't comforted.

'Go ahead.'

She went in. He followed and quietly closed the door behind him. He locked it.

Then he looked around.

'Beautiful,' he said. 'Your home is very lovely. You're a very lucky person, Carole.'

He motioned toward the living room.

'Let's sit down, okay? And then I want you to do something for me, all right?'

She took the chair near the fireplace and he took the couch, his gun resting along the armrest, still pointed more or less in her direction. He set the clipboard down and let the pencil roll across the heavy glass tabletop. He seemed at ease, very much in control.

He *was* in control.

He was male. He had a gun.

The world was filled with them.

She thought about the magnum in the drawer upstairs. The drawer was a million miles away. The drawer was on another planet, really.

'What?' she said. Her voice sounded husky, strange to her. 'You want me to do what?'

He crossed his legs. At home here.

'I'd like you to call Mr Edwards at work. Tell him that something's come up and you need him home right away.'

'How do you know about . . . Mr Edwards?'

'Never mind how I know. Or who I know or what I know. The point is just to call him.'

'He can't just pick up and leave.'

He smiled. 'Of course he can. And he will – you know he will. You also know *why* he will. Please, Carole. No games. No silliness. No make-believe. It's okay to call you Carole, isn't it? And Mr Edwards is Lee. Carole and Lee. And you can call me Wayne.'

'What do you want with . . . Mr Edwards?'

He frowned.

'You're asking an awful lot of questions, Carole. You know what this is?'

He pointed the gun.

'It's a snub-nose Smith and Wesson .38. Got any guns in the house?'

'No.'

He smiled. 'Sure you do. A house this big, this pretty? Look at all you've got worth stealing. Probably upstairs, right? We'll have a look around later.

'But now I want you to call Lee for me. It's okay if you sound a little upset. You *do* sound upset, you know that? He'll just get here faster that way. Upset's fine. Where's the phone?'

She glanced toward the table next to the sofa.

'Okay, good. Call him.'

She stood. The room swam. Her legs felt like cardboard. She had to sit down again. She needed to use the bathroom, suddenly she needed it badly. And there was every possibility that she was going to throw up then and there.

'Take it easy,' he said. 'I know this is stressful for you. Take a breath. Take a good, deep breath. Good. There. Now another one. Good, there you go. Excellent. Now try again.'

She got up.

'Oh and by the way,' he said. 'No nine-one-ones or anything, okay? I'm not stupid.'

Her legs still felt shaky but they held her. She got to the phone and dialed. But she must have gotten the number wrong because the voice on the other end belonged to a little girl of maybe six or seven and there were no little girls at Lee's office, for God's sake, so she hung up.

'What's the problem?'

'I dialed wrong,' she said.

He seemed to find that hilarious. 'Jesus, Carole! You're a *mess*! Calm down, will you? Come on. Give it another try.'

'Can I . . . do you mind if I use the bathroom?'

'After you call.' He laughed again. 'It'll add that element of . . . *urgency*.'

She dialed again. This time she got it right. His secretary put her on hold for a moment and then he was on the line and she was telling him to please come home, please Lee, please, come home right away. She was begging again. While the man Wayne stared at her across the room and tapped his knee with the barrel of the .38.

She heard Lee asking her what the hell was happening and why she was crying.

She hadn't even known she was crying. She hadn't been aware.

Hurry, she said.

She hung up the phone and turned to the man on the couch. The man was probably ten years younger than she was. Thin. Wiry. Without the gun the man might not have been bad looking in an ordinary sort of way but the gun reminded her of Howard, the gun had the dark potent magic to deform the man and turn him ugly.

'What . . . what do we do now?' she asked.

He shrugged. Then he smiled. It was an oddly friendly smile.

'We get to use the bathroom,' he said.

Eleven

'You,' Lee said.

He knew the man immediately.

His memory for faces was good. Besides, as bartenders go the guy was memorable. He poured short and cheap and used far too much ice and never bought a round no matter how long you sat there. But for the life of him he couldn't figure him here in this house. It was like seeing a movie star in Hoboken, New Jersey. He didn't fit.

'What's going on? What are you doing here?'

The man just smiled and looked at Carole and sipped a tumbler of scotch. This one not so short at all.

'Mr Lock and I have been talking,' said Carole.

He looked at her. She hadn't looked this bad, this strung out, since the Notch.

'He knows everything, Lee.'

He couldn't have heard correctly. Nobody knew. Not even the police. They'd spoken to no one. It was impossible.

'Say that again?'

'He knows everything.'

He could see she was working hard at keeping herself under control. She sat with her legs crossed tight and her arms folded. Her face had that pinched look again. She was not drinking.

Well fuck this. He was.

He put down the briefcase and went to the bar. The Glenfiddich was out. The guy was drinking Glenfiddich over ice. Which said something about the type of guy he was. Lee poured his neat. The shake had reached into his hands all of a sudden, into his shoulders.

'You want to explain that to me?' he said, not to Carole but to the man.

'I saw it,' he said. 'I watched you. The baseball bat. The rock. The clean-up. All of it. I was right over your heads, up on a ridge there. Then I went down to the stream. He'd already moved quite a ways, actually, by the time I got down there. I pushed him out into the middle of the stream. Figured I'd help out a little.'

The whisky burned only slightly. The man was enjoying this, leaning forward, smiling.

'So what do you want? Money? How much?'

The man just looked at him. He seemed amused.

'Company, Lee,' said the man. 'All I want is company.'

He was thinking about the gun in the drawer. He was thinking about ways to kill the man.

'I don't get it,' he said.

'Carole says that it was her husband you killed and that he deserved it, that there was no other way. That you'd tried the police and that you'd tried to bribe him off with money. I believe her. I see no reason not to. I know plenty of people who deserve to die. Plenty, believe me. But I don't really care about any of that now.'

He leaned forward even further, intent. The black snub-nose pistol gripped tightly in his lap.

'What I want to know from you, Lee, what I want to know right now is what it was *like*. See, I want you to tell me. I've really . . . *wondered*, you know?' He smiled.

Lee looked deep into the smile and something in there scared him. Money, blackmail he could understand. It was the way of the world. It was business. But this was crazy. *What was it like?* They were in the company of some weird sick freak here.

'Who knows?' the man said. 'Maybe I'll want to try it.'

Lee just looked at him. And the man must have thought that he didn't understand.

'Killing somebody,' he said.

Lee's whisky glass was empty. He put it down on the sideboard. He glanced at Carole. From the look of her he guessed they were thinking along the same lines.

He took a breath. Go on, he thought. Say it. Better the demon you know than the one you don't know.

'Are you talking about us?' he said.

Lock laughed. Like this was very funny to him.

'God, no! Never! You're missing the point entirely. I want to *know* you guys. I *respect* you guys. What you did took incredible balls, *incredible* balls! I'm in *awe* of you two guys. I mean, look how *well* you did it. Even forgetting the little assist from me. I mean, you're probably the *last* two people I'd want to kill. Honest!'

The man looked down.

Beastie was nuzzling his pants leg.

'Hey, kitty!'

He reached down and scratched her ear.

67

He didn't know shit about cats. Probably didn't like them either. He scratched her much too hard and too vigorously. Beastie shot him a look and trotted away.

He relaxed into the sofa. Sipped his whisky.

'Look, let's begin at the beginning. You tell me all about it, I mean all about yourselves, and I'll tell you all about me. We'll understand one another in no time. You'll see. Only, let's do it in my car, okay? We'll go for a little ride, the three of us. It's going to be a really nice night tonight. We'll have a little dinner, take a little ride. And you can drive, Lee. You see? I even trust you with my Volvo. Come on, It'll be fun.'

He stood up, the gun in a neutral position at his side. Lee found the word he'd been looking for to describe the man. The guy was *cheerful*. Relentlessly cheerful.

'Come on,' he said. 'I'll buy you a drink. I bet you could use one.' He laughed. 'I bet I scared the beejeesus out of you! Right, Carole?'

Carole looked at Lee. He nodded.

She stood up.

'I'll go get my jacket,' she said. She moved toward the stairs.

'That's where the gun is, isn't it?' said Lock. 'Upstairs.'

Carole stopped and turned. 'What gun?'

He grinned. 'Come on. I know you've got one somewhere. It's up there, right? Well, bring it on down. The more the merrier!'

He turned to Lee. 'What is it? Colt? Magnum?'

And then looked back to Carole.

'Please, guys,' he said. 'We're all gonna be friends here. I know you don't exactly believe me on that yet but you will. I'm making you a solemn promise. I'm not going to hurt you, either of you, as long as you don't do something where I have to.

'Now Lee's right here not five feet away from me. I'm a very good shot. And I bet you're not, Carole. So just go on up and bring it down. I trust you. Go ahead.'

Lee watched her ascend the stairs. There was a slouch to her strong back that was depressingly familiar.

She looked like she'd been beaten again, felt the pounding of rough hands against soft flesh.

She was not going to try something. Not now. In her place he wouldn't have either.

They walked to the car. Lock had Carole's jacket draped over the magnum and it was trained on the center of Lee's back. The .38 was in Lock's back pocket. Just until you get to know me better, he'd said again. And apologized.

He'd admired the magnum greatly and at length. Would they mind if they took it with them?

That was fine with Lee. One more gun meant one more opportunity. Though so far the guy had covered all his bases neatly.

He figured it couldn't last. The guy would make a slip. They'd be able to get to one of the guns and then they'd face him down. He felt sure that faced down, Lock would fold.

And then what? he thought.

They couldn't just run to the police and turn him in.

Lock knew.

And in a crunch Lee had no doubt that he would tell anybody and everybody exactly *what* he knew.

The way out, of course, was to kill him. And kill him as soon as possible, before anybody could associate him and Carole with the man. While as far as anybody else knew they were still all strangers to each other.

Could he do it? He felt pretty certain he could. The only question was how.

It was not like Howard. This time he wouldn't hesitate. The man was a lizard, crawled out from under a rock.

Take your time, he thought. Think and keep thinking. And when you see something, *move.*

'You parked pretty far away,' he said.

Wayne smiled. 'Well, I didn't want to arouse any suspicions.'

That was good. That was *very* good. *He didn't want to arouse any suspicions.* They were walking four blocks through their own neighborhood, curbs empty every place you looked from their house all the way over to the Nichols' house, they were walking all this way to get into a car that could have been parked right out in front of their own driveway.

He didn't want to arouse any suspicions.

It's a good sign, he thought. The guy is not all that organized.

He's got blank spots.

Maybe he could use that.

'I forgot to feed the cats,' said Carole.

'Don't worry about it,' Lock said. 'We won't be gone that long. You drive, Lee. Okay?'

Lee had never met anybody who jumped so hard and fast at getting on a first-name basis.

It seemed important to him.

He got into the driver's seat, Carole silent beside him, looking as though she were hardly breathing.

Lock – correction, *Wayne* – climbed in back.

'So. Where to, Wayne?' he said.

He could see the smile brighten through the rear-view mirror.

'Just drive, Lee,' he said. 'Just drive.'

Twelve

Rule knocked. Number 2211 again. Twice in two days was his personal record for the place but he had a feeling he might be breaking that soon.

The BMW and Edwards' Porsche sat in the driveway.

There was nobody home.

He tore a leaf off his notepad and wrote, *Important, please call* with his name and number and wedged it tight between the door and casing trim.

The stained glass sidelights on the door made him think of the dolls' house – he'd done those sidelights in clear thick plastic – and the dolls' house made him think of Chrissie and Ann in California.

What time was it there, three o'clock? Ann would still be at her computer at the bank and Chrissie would be just getting out of school, going to her grandmother's house or maybe to the *Y* afterschool program.

There was a time he'd have known which.

It was no big thing, but he missed knowing.

Get off it, he thought.

You're obsessing.

He walked down the stairs. He gazed through the windows of the Porsche and the BMW. There was nothing much to see. The Porsche was neater than her BMW, which surprised him a little. Just a newspaper folded on the dashboard – while Carole's car had cigarette wrappers, a crumpled-up piece of notepaper, something that looked like a stepped-on breath mint and a face-up Jefferson quarter on the floor and a small brown paper bag flattened on the passenger seat. Both cars were locked.

He stepped past the hedges to the front bay window and looked inside. He could see two glasses on the sideboard in the living room, an indentation in the couch where somebody'd been sitting pretty recently and a brown leather briefcase set down in the middle of the room. It was not the usual place to leave a briefcase but apart from that things looked perfectly normal. In one of the glasses ice was melting.

He'd just missed them.

It was beginning to get dark. The investigation up at the Notch would be winding down. Covitski, who'd arrived an hour after Rule, was running the show up there now. He'd be calling in shortly.

71

It was probably not worth waiting for them to return.

He wondered whose car they were in. Who was keeping them company.

The coroner's report on Howard wouldn't be on his desk until tomorrow morning earliest. He'd asked for a hurry-up. He even stood a chance of getting one because it was impossible to tell at this point if they were dealing with accidental death or homicide and there were not all that many deaths under questionable circumstances in this county. The coroner's office would be interested in this one the same way a computer nerd would be interested in some exotic little bug in his machine. Something challenging for a change.

Rule was rooting for simple death by misadventure. Carole Gardner had enough problems. Even if it turned out that Howard was killed by his goddamn ski instructor for zigging when he should have zagged any homicide investigation would inevitably start with her. They'd put her through the wringer. They had to.

Meaning he had to.

And he didn't feel like doing that.

He realized that in some ways this was personal. That money aside, Carole reminded him of Ann. He even thought they looked a little alike in some ways. It was probably why Ann was on his mind so much today. At least partly that.

There were similarities. Ann's husband, Chrissie's father, had been a heavy drinker too. And abusive. He worked on a smaller scale than Howard. But then most people did.

In her case it was mental abuse mostly. Ann hadn't the brains to do a damn thing as far as he was concerned and Chrissie was just an accident of chemistry that in his view had turned into a demanding, whining little brat. When he was drunk he struck out. He hit. He did that a time or two.

And then one night he sent his daughter reeling across the kitchen head-first into the refrigerator door.

Ann packed their bags and that was that.

For sheer innovative nastiness Howard Gardner made Ann's husband look like a punk but there were enough similarities between them so that he sympathized with the woman.

Enough so that he wanted this fall of Gardner's to be the final miscalculation of a guy with enough alcohol in his blood to fuel the Concorde. And nothing more.

The coroner's report would either say that or it wouldn't. Until then there wasn't much to do except head on back and wait for Covitski's return and, hopefully, Carole's call. She'd never failed to return his messages in the past. He had no reason to suspect this was any different except for two cars sitting lonely in the driveway and a briefcase in the middle of the living-room floor.

And the fact that this time Howard was dead.

He considered that. All the way back to the station he considered it.

Howard was dead and you could say he'd been courting death for quite a while in various ways, and at 2211 there was nobody home.

What did you do, Carole? he thought.

Just what in hell did you do?

Thirteen

They were on Interstate 89 heading toward Montpelier before she really started listening to what he was saying and even then it came upon her slowly, something about his mother and neighbors and an old house over on Sycamore and two old men he'd read about in Waterbury who'd faced one another with shotguns after one of them took a shot at the other's cat and now both of them were in the hospital probably dying. And so on.

Until then either she couldn't concentrate or she'd successfully blocked him out – she wasn't sure which. All she could hear was herself speaking quietly inside her own skull. What she was saying was that they were in deep and terrible trouble. That it was over now. That there was no alternative left now but to get to Rule and tell him everything. It was the only way to get rid of the man.

Already, in just this hour or so since he strolled up the driveway into her life, telling Rule would be a relief. Arrest seemed in every way preferable to his company.

And to his knowledge.

She felt unclean because of his knowledge. So filthy she wanted to cry.

She listened to the voice inside her head and it sounded dull and flat and wise as doom. It was leaden, it was enervating. As though even her blood were moving more slowly, thickening inside her.

The man had been inevitable.

It was only right, wasn't it, that somebody had found out?

It was only justice.

They'd killed a man.

Never mind that Howard was evil. Evil was only her opinion of him. The voice inside her said it was a highly educated opinion but so what?

What right did she have?

She had grown up knowing right from wrong down to the letter. She had learned it, she thought, the hard way. Sometimes she thought that as a child she had struggled to learn.

Knowing it was a contract. It bound you to the rest of the human race. She believed in it.

She'd broken that contract.

74

In some ways she deserved the man.

Justice. Guilt. Depression.

The three held hands, played ring-around-the-roses inside her. Became one and the same word almost. One heavy black form which shapeshifted within her until she could feel nothing but weight, density, and darkness.

Ring-around-the-roses.

The reference was to the Black Death, wasn't it? To the plague.

Filthy.

Let it come, she thought. Fine, let it happen. I'll let go of it.

Let it all be over.

She could almost hear the tumbrels moving through the streets. She deserved them.

'Pull up! Quick! *Pass her!*'

The voice jolted her.

She felt the car lurch forward as Lee obeyed. Behind her Wayne was pounding on his seat, excited. Lee looked confused, like he didn't know exactly what the point was here.

She glanced beyond him out the driver's side window. Saw that they were gaining on a blue Ford wagon, passing it on the right. The driver was a woman, profiled dim and grey in the dusk.

Wayne rolled down his window.

They were passing slowly, gradually nosing past her.

'Give her the horn.'

'What?'

'I said give her your horn. Use the horn!'

Lee hit it with his fist, two short bursts. The woman glanced over. Carole had the impression of both youth and age at once – a young mother maybe. It would fit the way she looked. Baggy sweatshirt. Hair pulled back in a pony tail. Driving a wagon.

Carole turned and saw Wayne lean out the window motioning to the driver. Pointing down at her right rear tire.

So that was it.

Something was wrong with the tire.

The woman saw him, understood, gave him a worried smile and nodded. She slowed, turned the wheel and fell back into the lane behind them.

'Pull over.'

Lee was frowning. 'Why? What for?'

'The tire. She's gonna need help with that.'

Carole watched the wagon stop along the narrow shoulder. Lee pulled over.

'Come on,' said Wayne.

The woman was opening her door, getting out of the car.

The magnum was up and pointing at Lee across the seat.

Lee opened his door, put one foot outside it and so did she on her side.

'You going to take that with you, Wayne?' he said.

Wayne laughed. He put the gun down beside him on the car seat.

'Just remember the other one,' he said. 'Okay?' He patted his back pocket.

The woman was moving around behind her car, looking first at the rear tire on the driver's side and then walking around to the other.

Cars whooshed by as they approached her. Some had their headlights on. It was getting close to dark.

The woman looked up at them, puzzled. She was blonde, a little overweight, but pretty.

'I don't see . . .'

Carole found herself glancing through the woman's back-seat window. She didn't know what she was looking for. A car seat for a child maybe.

There wasn't any.

No kids' stuff in the rear compartment either. A tire. A checkered quilt. That was all.

For some reason she felt relieved. She didn't know why.

Not right away.

It took her only a moment to check inside the woman's car but when she looked up again Wayne was two steps ahead of them when he'd been a step behind her only a second ago, he'd moved that fast, and Lee was lurching back. She nearly stumbled into him.

The look on his face was shocked. Frightened.

And the gun was up and firing.

Her name was Deanna Morris. A file clerk and typist for a Barstow law firm taking what she called a 'mental health day' after six grueling days and nights helping to prepare a brief on a child-molestation case, The People vs. Sunnybrook Day Care, a detestable case to her way of thinking because she was sure that the people at Sunnybrook were guilty, and she herself was five months pregnant by her husband Carl, her own burgeoning motherhood making their defense of Sunnybrook's owners all the more repulsive – but it was a job. She knew that this would be her last 'mental health day' for a while. The pregnancy would probably consume the rest of her sick-days and maybe then some.

She was on her way to meet Carl at his construction site, to pick him up after work because the Chevy's driver-side window had popped off its track again and the car was at the shop. They were going to have dinner. Probably Italian.

Payments on the house were reasonable. So were payments on the two cars.

She and Carl were happy together now that the lean times were over and they both, thank God, were working finally. For their son – the sonogram had told them it was a boy – there would be comfort and stability, at least for the foreseeable future.

She was five feet three inches tall.

The man with the gun was much taller, perhaps five-nine.

So the first bullet entered high through the deltoid muscle of her shoulder, plowed through her pectoral muscles to the sternum, chipped the sternum and exited through the ribs of her back.

She heard herself scream and the flat report of the gun simultaneously.

By then the man had shot her a second time.

Instinctively she had thrown up her left hand toward him to ward him off, and turned her back. The first bullet's impact spun her around even further so that her back was square to him as he fired the second shot – and she was crouching a little, her fingers still splayed behind her like a discus thrower or a bowler at the peak of her backswing.

The shot tore away most of her left index finger before entering her back to the right of the vertebral column and scattering her kidneys out in front of her all across the tarmac. It looked like an open dog-food can had simply exploded out of her.

She fell sideways to her knees, catching herself with the palm of her right hand. She knelt there canted to the right trying to breathe. There was no pain, only amazement, horror at the awful thing she had witnessed the man do – and though she could not have phrased it, a raw yearning disappointment. A final scan for meaning that ended in senseless waste.

She was a realistic person, she had prided herself in that, and understood as she fell that her life, so full of purpose both mundane and far-reaching just seconds ago, had now suddenly entered into the realm of the useless and the ridiculous. A sock with a hole where the toes peeked through. A garden hose clogged all summer. A stewpot with no handles.

That was what she was.

That was what the gun had made of her.

A joke.

'*Eeeee*yah!'

Wayne was leaping along the shoulder like a crazed ape, like some fucking wide receiver who's just scored the winning touchdown.

'Jesus Christ! Did you *see* that?'

The woman's body slumped on its side. Lee smelled urine, shit, and gunpowder. Cars whizzed by. He could feel the warm thrusting breeze of their passing. One seemed to slow and then moved on.

'Come on. Get back in the car.' The gun was pointed at him. Then at Carole.

Then back at him again.

'Get into the car!'

They did as he said. There was no way he could get to the magnum. Wayne was too close. And Wayne was timing it perfectly. He had the rear door open, one foot in, and the .38 trained on Lee's back through the window until Lee got his own door open. Then he just slid inside. He held both guns now, the magnum pointed at Lee's ear and the. 38 at Carole.

'Drive!'

Lee waited for a break in the traffic and pulled away.

He looked through the rear-view mirror. The woman's station wagon receded behind him. Just beyond it one pale arm pointed toward the highway. The glint of a bracelet in the lights of an approaching car.

Why hadn't someone stopped?

Why weren't they stopping now?

'Put on your lights.'

He was aware of Carole sobbing beside him, her fist clenched tight to her mouth.

There were a million things to say and nothing worth saying. They drove in silence.

The silence buzzed and droned.

He drove and shook and gripped the wheel.

He adjusted the mirror so that Wayne was in the frame. It seemed important to have him there.

The look on his face was distant. The eyes glittered brightly, skittered in their sockets. Only the eyes moved. He could see the man relax into something and he could guess what Wayne was doing, that he was replaying the whole thing over in his mind.

He would want to do that.

Of course he would.

Lee had replayed Howard's death a few times too 'by now. The difference was he'd had no choice. They'd come unbidden. Images skewed so that it was he who was holding the rock, not Carole.

He saw it now.

He was driving badly. He knew that. As though the wheel had too much play in it suddenly. His lane seemed elusive. Passing cars were giving him a wide berth.

'We ought to . . . I should get off the highway,' he said.

'Huh?'

'I think I'm not doing so well here. Driving, I mean. We ought to go

78

somewhere. Stop. For a little while, anyhow. Give me a minute to . . . collect myself, you know?'

Wayne smiled.

'Yeah. Pretty fucking wild, wasn't it?'

He laughed and slapped his seat again. The .38 was gone from his hand. Either it was on the car seat beside him or he'd pocketed it.

'Okay. Sure. Take your next exit. You like McDonald's? Maybe we can find a McDonald's. Get some burgers. I'm sorry about that drink I promised. It'll have to wait. Okay?'

He and Carole exchanged glances.

'What?' said Wayne. 'You got a problem with that?'

'No. No problem.'

'I can't believe it. I can't believe I *fucking did it*. Jesus! You feel that way after?'

'What way?'

'Like everything's different. Like from now on, everything changes.'

'I don't know. Maybe.'

The exit was coming up. *Williamstown*, the sign said. He'd had no idea they'd come this far.

'So how did it feel? Watching me, I mean.'

'How did it feel?'

He pulled off onto the ramp. Slowed. He saw Carole turn, dry-eyed, *wild*-eyed, suddenly glaring at the man.

'It felt sickening,' she said. 'It felt sickening, you son of a bitch. You sick *bastard*!'

And then she was up on her knees on the car seat, leaning over, trying to pummel him with her fists, Wayne fending her off easily but in one hand he still held the magnum and Lee thought Jesus Christ the thing could go off right here inside the car and what the hell was she *doing*? Wayne was laughing, her blows completely ineffectual and she knew it, so she was going right over the seat after him, trying to climb right into the back, screaming, furious, calling him *bastard bastard bastard*.

He slowed where the ramp went into a curve, slid into the curve despite slowing, fishtailing, and then got beyond the curve on a straightaway and reached around. He found the back of her blouse at the neck with his hand and he grabbed it and pulled.

'Carole! For Chris*sake*!'

The man was still laughing, squealing, having a hell of a time with her, slapping her fists away with his open left hand and the barrel of the fucking gun and Lee pulled at her again, pulled hard.

And he guessed she was off balance because her head nearly went back into the windshield. Her right hand smacked the rear-view mirror and her back hit the dashboard hard enough so that the glove compartment popped open and wedged against her as she slid knees-first off the seat down onto the floor.

It hurt. You could see it on her face.

Too fucking bad.

A bullet would have hurt a whole lot more.

He was drifting almost to a stop now. Luckily there were no cars behind him.

'You all right?'

She nodded.

She wouldn't look at him.

She pulled herself up onto the seat and sat staring.

He adjusted the mirror.

Wayne was smirking at her, his eyes trying to bore into the back of her skull. It was just as well she didn't see them, he thought. It could start her up all over again.

He had a carful of goddamn lunatics here.

He glanced at the road ahead and then back at Wayne again. His face seemed to have softened in the instant he'd looked away.

'I understand, Carole,' he said. His voice was controlled, quiet. 'I frightened you. I'm sorry. I promise – it won't happen again.'

He leaned toward her. For a terrible moment it looked as though he were going to bury his face in her long dark hair.

'From now on,' he said, 'there'll be no surprises. Anything that happens, anything we do, I'll let you know in advance. Okay?'

Lee didn't think she was even listening to him. She said nothing. Just stared straight through the windshield at the road ahead.

Lee was listening, though.

And he heard the man's subtext loud and clear.

It was a warm humid night but his fingers on the wheel felt suddenly cold.

There were going to be more.

That was what he was saying. That was the subtext. The woman wasn't the last of them.

He was just beginning.

Fourteen

It was four days now and Susan was feeling bad for him.

She'd been thinking about Wayne all day on and off at work, damning herself for a fool after what he'd done to her but then remembering some of the things he'd said at other times and feeling sort of bad for him, feeling practically guilty.

About how his father, dead fifteen years now, had locked him up in the pickup while he hit the local taverns all day long sometimes. How he'd hustled Wayne's first and only dog off to the veterinarian. 'The dog's a bird-killer and he's got to die,' he'd said. Wayne's father had a thing about birds, feeders all over the place, and the dog had snapped the pinfeathers off a starling.

He'd had it rough with his father.

To hear Wayne talk his mother was practically a saint. But his father was another matter.

She wasn't excusing him. Not exactly. But she thought that it might be okay to give him a chance to explain himself. She hadn't the other day. She'd been far too scared and angry.

She knew that there were people who actually liked to do what Wayne had done to her. They did it all the time. There was even a name for it. They said when you couldn't breathe sometimes it made your orgasm better, stronger.

Hers had been pretty strong.

While it lasted. Until she got scared of him.

She could still remember the feel of his hands around her throat. She wasn't forgetting that.

Still . . .

She hadn't let him explain. It was possible he was just being sort of experimental. She could certainly make it clear to him that that wasn't her idea of fun.

She could at least give him a chance to talk to her about it.

It was hard to dial, though. Hard to know what to do.

She sat on the couch and watched the streetlight blinking erratically on and off across from her apartment. Obviously the bulb was going.

Probably she was crazy even to *think* about calling Wayne.

Because maybe he *wasn't* being experimental. There was that possibility too.

But there had been good times. Lots of them. Susan hadn't had all that many boyfriends, just a few, really, and none who were as thoughtful as Wayne could be when he wanted to. Who but Wayne would show up at the dentist's office thinking she might have had a bad reaction to the novocain and would maybe need a ride? Who would send her flowers on mother's day even though she was nobody's mother, God knows, calling it 'an investment in her future.' She'd laughed and said she was kind of a mother anyway, she was already mothering *him*, and he didn't take it badly – he'd laughed.

But there was truth to that too. The mother thing.

Maybe that was why she wanted to call him.

She was nobody's idea of a beauty. She'd been fat as a kid and traces of that tendency remained, especially around her butt and thighs. Her nose was a little too long. Her chin too weak. Oh, she knew how to attract a man if need be, she'd learned that much, all right, that wasn't the problem.

But she found that now she didn't much want to. There was something about Wayne which appealed to the care-giver in her, she guessed. Something that just didn't surface with most other men.

A need in him. A loneliness. Almost a hunger for some sort of connection.

She dialed his number.

She dialed four more times, thinking that there was probably no more solitary sound in the world than a telephone line that just rings and rings.

There was always the bar later. She could call him there if she wanted to.

She wondered if she'd want to.

She wondered if he'd already found somebody else. Somebody to replace her. It was only four days but it was possible. Wayne could be charming and he was pretty good looking even if, like most men, he didn't know how to dress in a way that would show him off well. At least she thought so.

If he'd found somebody, she wondered if she'd be willing to just let it go at that, to accept it, or if she'd want to go the extra mile and fight for him somehow.

She didn't know.

Maybe later she'd phone the bar.

She imagined Wayne feeling lonely. Missing her but too damn proud or too ashamed to call. She thought of him with another woman. It was hard to say which was worse.

Maybe she'd call.

She had plenty of time to think it over. Maybe she'd try. Maybe it was worth trying.

She really didn't know.

Fifteen

Covitski put down the phone and wearily shook his head. He stood up. His weight made that slow going.

'You're not gonna believe this,' he said to Rule. 'We got a shooting out on I-89. Lady in a station wagon. Is this piece-of-shit day never gonna end?'

Rule looked at him. 'You're going out there?'

'Hey. Like I got nothing to do, right?'

Rule knew what he meant. It had been a long day for both of them. Covitski had been out at the stream on the Gardner thing till six. They'd turned up nothing out there so it would all begin again tomorrow. Covitski had that to look forward to plus probably half a dozen other cases and now this.

Like everybody else these days they were understaffed, work jammed into every one of them like meat into so many sausage casings.

'Covitski, my heart goes out to you. I'm two cases shy of an even dozen, you know?' He flipped some pages in the Wourmouth file. 'And this one. I just *love* this one. Who the hell would ever think that a simple domestic dispute would blow up into so much goddamn paperwork?'

Covitski laughed. 'It happens. When you got a husband, you got his wife, you got his girlfriend, two cousins and an eighty-year-old drunken granddaddy all doing the disputing.'

'I guess. Anyhow, good luck. Who's the victim?'

Covitski consulted his pad.

'Morris, first name Deanna. Married. Husband's name is Carl. Two, maybe three slugs in her. Blonde, late twenties. Driving a blue '91 Ford wagon.'

'Any leads?'

'Nah. Nothing.'

'Yeah. Well, like I say, good luck.'

'Uh-huh.'

He was just out the door when the phone rang – his line. Rule picked it up anyway.

Most of his attention was still with the Wourmouth file until he heard what the guy had to say.

The man's voice was scared and jittery and Rule could read him instantly. The man wanted desperately to hang up. He couldn't bring himself to do that just yet. But he was working on it.

Which meant that Rule had to play this fish very carefully.

The man thought he saw a murder.

Or more precisely, the aftermath of one.

Rule took his name and number, coaxed it out of him slowly and gently, voice nice and even, soothing, got the location of what the guy had seen, a description of what the guy had seen, the time of day and all the details.

Once he'd calmed him down, the caller had a pretty good memory. Even took a partial, *GO* something, on the plate of a 1993 Volvo, color red, parked along the highway.

He described a thin, dark-haired man in a white shirt, medium build, early thirties, climbing into the back of the Volvo. There was another somewhat older man driving and a dark-haired woman sitting beside him. The woman wore her hair long. She was slim and attractive. The driver's hair was thinning.

Rule wrote it all down even though calls were taped routinely. Thanked the man and arranged to get a written statement from him in the morning.

Then thought, well. What have we got here?

Covitski had a break. That much was certain.

And maybe so did he.

It didn't *quite* add up. In fact it didn't add up at all on the face of it but he had a feeling when the man was describing the couple, the man and the woman, riding in front.

He got up and poured himself a cup of coffee, black and thick and nasty, into his Disneyland mug, souvenir of the Magic Kingdom, sunny California, and then he called Covitski.

Sixteen

'I want to do another one,' Wayne said. 'You want to help this time?'

Like he was talking about a second hand of gin.

'All I want to do is get out of here, Wayne,' said Lee. 'That's all either of us want. You know that.'

'Why? Look, we do one more and then I'll drop you somewhere. I'll go away. I swear.'

They sat in the McDonald's lot and she was listening to them, not believing this conversation, not believing anything *about* it, Wayne talking through bites of his quarter-pounder. The smell inside the car was sickening. Grease, onions. *Meat*.

She had the window open but there was no breeze. The night was still. The night cloyed.

Cars passed by on the way to the drive-in window.

Wayne sipped loudly through the straw. Iced tea with lemon.

She could call to someone. Someone passing by.

She could jump out of the car and run.

He'd shoot her. He'd shoot before her foot was even out the door. Before she was finished screaming.

He wouldn't mind a bit.

She wanted to cry. She wanted a gun.

She kept seeing the woman's death played out in front of her exactly as it had happened, down to the smallest detail. Index finger pumping blood. Eyes squinting shut – *see no evil*. Woman on her knees, draining out onto the tarmac. Balance sliding away. Slumping. Falling.

Crumpled. The woman a death-sack.

My God, that poor young woman.

'Then why not let us out right now?' Lee was saying. *Still trying to talk to him.* As though something about him might respond to the rational.

'Let us out right here. Then you go do . . . whatever it is you want to do.'

Wayne looked at him and shook his head as though Lee were somebody's idiot brother.

'Company,' he said through a mouthful of hamburger. 'Remember, Lee? *Company*. 'Member what I said? It's great having somebody around

86

who knows how you feel. It's the greatest thing in the world.' He laughed. 'Well, almost the greatest.'

'We don't have the slightest idea how you feel, Wayne.'

'Sure you do.'

He sounded almost shy. Something grotesquely innocent about the man. Like he was really just a little boy caught in some sin he had never comprehended in the first place. *Thou shalt not covet thy neighbor's wife* explained to a three-year-old. *Mommy? What's covet? What's neighbor?*

What's wife?

Except that he wasn't a little boy and the word in question here was simple.

The word was murder.

She thought of Howard. She still could almost feel the weight of the rock raised above her.

Simple? Was it really?

Yes, she thought. For her and for Wayne both, when you got right down to it, it was simple. She knew what she did. And so did Wayne. The trouble was he felt nothing but excitement over it, like a kid starring in his own home movie.

He doesn't feel.

He hasn't got a clue.

Listen to him.

'I mean,' he was saying. 'I know it's not the same for everyone. Everybody's different. I'm not saying you know *exactly* how I'm coming at this, Lee. I mean, it's not even necessary. But I kind of like the idea of you guys as *witnesses*, you know what I mean? In the old-time sense. Bearing witness, you know? That kind of thing. And hell, I couldn't ask for better witnesses. See, you've at least been there. You know what I'm going through to that extent at least.'

She couldn't help it. *Enough*, she thought.

'No,' she said. 'We don't. What *are* you going through, Wayne?'

Her voice sounded every bit as cold and mean to her as she'd meant it to be. He didn't seem to notice.

'It's amazing,' he said. 'I know you're still mad at me, Carole. And I don't blame you because, let's face it, I did, I scared you. But I know you know what I'm talking about even if you won't admit it because you felt it too, I saw you with that rock and you had to feel it. See, here you are, you're doing what you were meant to do. Everything's *right*. You were *meant* to get rid of Howard. It felt *right* to get rid of Howard because Howard was such a son of a bitch, and at the same time it was the most important, most fucking expressive thing you ever did in your life. Am I right? I mean, what do you compare it to? Skiing? Sex? A European vacation?'

He laughed. 'It's ridiculous! There's no comparison with *anything*.'

He sat quiet for a moment.

'I think it's a secret,' he said. 'I think it's just this great big secret they keep from us. That they don't want us to know about unless maybe there's a war on or something and then, sure, they want you to know so you'll line up and do it and go on doing it and enjoy yourself all to hell. But otherwise they keep it from you. It's *their* secret. About how fucking good it feels. Y'know?'

There was no point debating with him.

There was no point talking at all. Wayne exhausted her.

She watched the cars pull up to the window. Kids dating. Families. Friends. Mac and a Coke and a large fries, please. All so terribly normal. Outside the car the whole wide world was normal. Or – who knew? — maybe *this* was normal, maybe cars were filled with lunatics all across America.

What rough beast . . .

All of them having conversations just like this one.

She thought of Howard's fists. Howard had exhausted her too.

She knew you could get used to anything.

When you did, it became normal.

She wondered if it had puzzled Lee's secretary at all that he hadn't returned to the office, that he hadn't called in.

She could hope so.

It was dark. The amber overhead lights in the parking lot blazed through a light fog. The lot looked like sundown on the day after World War III. A nuclear sky. Beyond the lot she could see headlights shooting by over a black unilluminated highway.

She needed to get to a phone. To call Rule. Somebody.

Confession would be fine. Normal.

She heard him crinkling up the McDonald's wrapper and stuffing it into the bag.

'Please. Let us *go*,' she said. 'Let us leave.'

Even exhausted it was worth a try.

He was quiet. He even seemed to give it thought.

'No,' he said. 'I don't want to do that. You've got to look at it from my point of view, Carole. I'm sorry. One more. It's very important to me. And then, maybe.'

'You can't do this, Wayne. You killed an innocent woman.'

He laughed. 'Of course I can. Hey, just look at us. See, that's what they never tell you. Anybody can. *Everybody* can.

'It's a free country.'

They were back on 89 South. Wayne wanted them to cross the New Hampshire border into Hanover.

What's in Hanover? Lee asked.

'Dartmouth,' Wayne shrugged, as though that explained something. And Lee thought, yes – Dartmouth. A college town, with plenty of cops around.

It might not be such a bad idea.

'I know what you're thinking,' Wayne said. He could actually *feel* him grinning in back of him. He was getting to be able to *sense* the guy. 'You're thinking that once we get there you can ram us into a tree or something, call attention to us somehow. Am I right?'

The guy was crazy but he was no fool. Though sideswiping a parked car somewhere in the center of town was more what Lee had in mind.

'But think, Lee. Think. Remember what I said? About you two guys being the last two people in the world I'd want to hurt?' He laughed. 'Well, it's true. You're the *last* two people. See?'

Mood-swings were running second-by-second inside the guy. The voice went intent and serious now.

'I'd consider that betrayal. Wouldn't you? I'd shoot, Lee. And I wouldn't stop shooting. I'd empty this fucking gun into both of you and I wouldn't give it another thought.'

Then he laughed. 'Hey, what have I got to lose, you know?'

What indeed.

Lee thought he'd known a little something about losing until he met Wayne. But Wayne was working a different strata entirely.

Lee had been born a war-baby, almost a year to the day after Hiroshima. His mother had died of bone cancer when he was six. He remembered a grey-faced woman barely able to turn and relieve her bedsores for fear of breaking yet another bone. His father had done his best afterwards.

He came of age, as they say, in the late sixties. He was going to school in Boston when Flower Power hit the streets of Beacon Hill and for three months that summer, the summer of '67, Summer of Love, the same wild optimism seemed to waft over everybody who lived there like a blessing, like a kind of permanent LSD-high of the soul, getting into your blood whether or not you were actually dropping the stuff.

They were kids. By sheer force of *style* they were going to change the world. Brand-new tie-dyed apostles carrying the Word to their pagan, world-weary elders. And of course the word was Love.

When the summer was over Lee began a two-year fling with teaching, impressing on his high school kids whenever the opportunity arose the same simple and to him obvious notions he'd embraced upon the Hill. Along with plenty of others it took him time to catch on to the fact that anger, manipulation and greed had already co-opted those notions and twisted them out of recognition.

It had happened so fast. Love was Fury – fury at the shootings at Kent State, at the death of Martin King. Getting high was bad dope and burnout. Peace was going to war with War, getting whacked by a riot stick on some Peace March because that pimply twenty-year-old kid at the head of the line who read himself to sleep with *Das Kapital* and whacked off to the poems of Mao decided that it would be an act of keen political savvy to firebomb a cop car and get some heads busted in time for the nightly news.

He thought it was Roger Corman who said right around then that if he could somehow get the word *Losers* into the title of every one of his films then they'd all make a million bucks. He had it right. They were all losers, from then on, failed idealists who had seen the clear pure light that summer and then had seen it come to nothing.

He'd gotten into drugs. Screwed his way to oblivion. Then swapped drugs for booze. Watched his father die.

And then said, finally, fuck it. By then there were Right-to-Lifers on the streets telling the world exactly what to do with their bodies and souls.

Fuck it.

He'd gotten into real estate. The art of selling too much land for too much money to people who would eventually allow him to sell it again for even more money to people who couldn't afford it in the first place.

He'd gotten into that.

And later, Carole.

You couldn't change the world anymore, at least not for the better, but you could change somebody's world and he'd settled for that. Even with what they'd done – what they'd irrationally and beyond hope felt *driven* to do, he saw that now – even with the nightmares and the memory he would probably have forever he wasn't unhappy with the decision.

So Wayne sits back and says, *What have I got to lose?*

Lee asked himself the same question.

For him the answer was easy. That was the difference between the two of them.

Life. Liberty. And don't forget the fucking Pursuit of Happiness.

He had already killed a man to hold onto these things and to hold onto her. He didn't regret it. Even though they were going to get caught now one way or another, he'd taken his shot. So it didn't work out. So what. You didn't give up. You still wanted to make it work somehow. You still plugged away at it because you never knew. You didn't drop dead for anybody.

He'd admit to having come by a certain coldness over the years, a certain distance. To the best of his capacity to love he did love Carole. Of that he was quite certain. It wasn't as though he was in this for the money and the comfort.

The problem was that he'd found out along the way, through a pretty long string of lovers, that you could burn out on passion and romance the same way you could burn out on bad dope or optimism or any other damn thing. It happened. And once it happened it was forever. So that then, even when something indisputably good came along, you maintained a kind of reserve.

Not that you didn't mine it for everything it was worth. Sure you did. But you stayed a little aloof from it too. Because mines had a tendency to come crumbling down in the course of time and when they did it was a whole lot better to be sitting on top of one than to get caught in the dark deep inside.

So answer the question, he thought.

What have you got to lose?

Whatever was left.

That was what.

And that was not nothing.

The sign said *Hanover Dartmouth University* and he pulled off onto 91. They were close to town.

He'd try to find a way to get rid of Wayne. He'd look hard for that. But he wasn't going to die trying.

You could plead temporary insanity to killing Howard and if the lawyer was good enough you might even make it stick.

You couldn't plead a damn thing to a bullet.

The woman had fallen not three feet away from him. He could see her wedding ring.

If Wayne was really smart enough and careful enough and if he really wanted to stay with them, then Lee guessed that he was staying.

The guns said so. And what the guns said was always right. It was the way of the world.

The hero in him had died long ago.

Rest in peace.

Tommy Braun was walking up Allen Street, heading up to the Balloon where there were potted plants in the window and the drinks were too expensive, he hated the place, but he wasn't going to be drinking any beers there anyway, he was just returning these three terrific copies of *Taboo* to Greg McCallum who washed their dishes in back, #4, #5, and the *Taboo Especial*. He'd read them each a couple of times and thought he liked #4 the best because of the Moebius *Eye of the Cat* and the S. Clay Wilson. But the other issues were pretty hot too.

It was warm out, much too warm to rush. So he took his time. Knobby knees poking out through the holes in his jeans. Wire-rim glasses mended with electricians' tape. The three oversized paperback comics swinging gently along at the end of his arm.

It would probably have amused him that because of the books and the glasses the guy in the Volvo mistook him for a student. Tommy cordially hated students – who all seemed to have more money than they knew what to do with, who made beer a whole lot more expensive than it needed to be and the availability of dateable women damn near nonexistent.

He was about to turn the corner, thinking that maybe he could get Greg to part with his collection of *Cry For Dawn* for a few days, when the car slowed down beside him and the guy leaned out and Tommy thought they were going to ask him directions.

He stopped, nearly always ready to be helpful directing somebody even when it was a student doing the asking. He was good at directions. He had a perfect sense of north, south, east and west and he knew the streets and roads for miles around.

He saw the gun only for a moment, bright silver shining thing in the streetlight, before the slug from the .357 magnum exploded through the right lens of his glasses, turning the lens to powder, liquefying the eye itself and thundering up through his cerebrum and out through the back of his head like a runaway train hurtling back through the parking lot behind him.

He fell, and the books fell and the binding broke on *Taboo* #4. His favorite.

To know this would have upset him.

He respected books more than he respected most of the people he knew and was always very careful with loaners.

'You're crazy! You're fucking crazy! Let me *out* of here!'

'Nobody moves!'

He had the gun pressed hard into the back of her neck and she was trying to get away from it but she couldn't find the goddamn button on the console that would unlock the door and the barrel of the gun, the sharp sight of the gun kept jabbing at her.

Jump! Jump!

'You stay where the fuck you *are*, Carole! You stay where you are!'

'Carole! Please! Hey. Don't . . .'

Lee was just trying to drive, trying to get the car around the corner, doing what Wayne had told him to do, trying to stay calm and calm her too because there was nothing they could have done to stop it and nothing they could do now and she knew that, nobody around, not a cop in sight and she *knew that but she had to get out*. This was madness. She had to!

Then Wayne's hand was in her hair, hurting her, pulling her head back, the gun pressed deep into her cheek.

'Drive! Drive, Goddammit!'

She could still hear the sound, the massive single flat tone, it roared in her head so that she could barely hear him or even her own voice it was so loud, a huge rolling note of thunder within the tiny car that now to her was suddenly so much smaller than it had been only a second ago, the car filled with a physical weight of sound that crowded them into corners like the hand of some sick invisible god pressing them apart and filling the spaces between them with pain and shock.

She could smell the powder – thick, rich, biting, drifting from the barrel of the gun. The scent of death fast and sure working its way into her through her nose through her mouth through her eyes bringing tears to her eyes, working its way in.

'Turn here. Back to 91. Do it!'

The boy was just a boy. Just a kid. Who would care about him? Who would regret?

Who would know?

'Take it back to 89 North.'

'Back?' Lee looked confused now as well as shaken.

'Yeah. Back.'

'I don't . . .'

'Don't worry about it. Just drive. Stay nice and calm, Lee, and drive. You're doing a fine job.'

He took the gun off the back of her neck.

He settled in.

Traffic was light. No sirens wailed through the night. No flashing lights. No high-speed pursuit.

No punishment.

And no redemption.

It was as though it had never happened.

The boy was there. And then he wasn't there. They had never even been to this town.

She thought she was going crazy, that this was what it was like.

For a long time no one spoke.

How long? An hour? She didn't know.

She felt sure an hour had passed. Maybe more. Her ears were still ringing, she could still feel the pressure inside them. She could still smell the faint reek of powder. She wondered if the gun had damaged her hearing permanently. She could almost wish it had.

Headlights. The road ahead. Nothing more. They were back on I-89. The traffic was heavier and Lee was going slowly. Cars passed them.

Cars all filled with strangers.

She could almost feel him drifting away, dreaming behind her in the back there. Dreaming awake, not sleeping. They were not going to get that lucky. Running the whole evening through like a movie on a VCR. *Play. Slow-frame. Stop-action.*

She hated him.

She had never hated anybody before. Not as far as she could remember. Not even her father. And there might have been good reason for that.

She had not even hated Howard – though God knows there was plenty of anger, plenty of fury. But mostly she'd been afraid of Howard, afraid of how he made her feel. Helpless. Lost. Trapped. As though she were on a dark flight of stairs leading nowhere going up, endlessly up, tiring and finally falling to her knees, falling over and over again, going nowhere.

That was why he died. Because he wouldn't go away.

So that what he made her feel wouldn't go away either.

But this man.

This man she hated.

She discovered that hating was physical, it was *action*, not simply feeling. There seemed to be nothing passive about it. It took energy, concentration. She sat there and worked the hate as you'd work a piece of clay, pushing, pulling it into the shape of something stark and real and recognizable, then molding it down soft again *so that he would never see it and never know*, then bringing it alive again into sharp definition.

As the headlights of cars drifted by, their drivers unseeing, unknowing.

She was masked. Veiled.

There was no place to take the hate so she held it tight and waited.

'This exit,' he said.

Off the ramp was a Comfort Inn. New and brightly lit.

'In here,' he said.

'Here?'

'That's right. Keep on going past the bar, see it there? And into the lot behind.'

There were only three cars parked in front of the two rear tiers of units. At this time of year business would be light. Even in front of the bar and restaurant area she'd only seen half a dozen cars.

'Park anywhere in here.'

Lee pulled in and stopped about midway down the line.

'Give me the keys,' said Wayne. Lee handed them over. She turned and saw that Wayne had her jacket again and had it draped over the magnum.

'Rest stop,' he grinned.

94

They got out and he walked them to the back of the car. He had the gun pointed at Lee while he used the car keys on the trunk and took out a small brown imitation leather suitcase. He closed the trunk and dug into his pocket. He grinned at them again and dangled another set of keys. The chain said Comfort Inn.

'You *planned* this?'

'Always think ahead, Lee. Here. It's right upstairs here.'

He pocketed the car keys, lifted the suitcase and walked them up the stairs ahead of him, careful to stay well behind. It was probably good he was careful. The urge to kick back at him or even fall back into him and push him down at all costs, to watch him fall and bleed, was like the taste of licorice in her mouth.

'To your right there. Number 233.'

He opened the door. They stepped inside.

Two queen-sized beds, a television, a desk and dresser. A bathroom with a door in back. A mirrored sink and dressing area.

The usual.

'Sit down, guys.'

They sat beside one another on the far bed nearest the dressing area. The air in the room was still and musty.

The bed felt good. The bed felt fine. She realized that she was very tired. She could have slept on the bed in a minute. Curled up with her hate and gone to sleep. She could have slept for hours.

He closed the checkered curtains. Flicked on the overhead light. He put the suitcase down on the other bed and opened it in front of them, turned it toward them so they could see.

And whatever drowsiness she felt disappeared. Fled her instantly.

She saw the steel gleam of handcuffs atop the jumbled clothing, saw the pliers, the kitchen knife, the hammer, the thick ball of wire. She saw the look on his face that was not smiling now nor even amused but serious, and the gun that was raised and pointed at them.

'What do you want?' she said.

His look said it was obvious.

'I want more,' he said.

Seventeen

Rule thought sometimes that his life had devolved into work, beer and the tv set, with the weekly visit to Marty and the occasional pause to eat its only variations. Now and then he could rouse himself to visit the dolls' house out in the garage. But work on the dolls' house seemed to have lost much of its juice since they'd gone. Or maybe he was just reluctant to see it over. For whatever reason it languished.

Tonight he was sitting down with his second Amstel Lite watching Cinemax. The movie was Rutger Hauer in *Blind Fury*.

Hauer was sightless but in perfect touch with the Force or whatever it was and he was moving through a wheat field. He had just finished dispatching one of the bad guys – who were chasing his buddy's kid – with a single thrust from the sword he kept hidden in his cane. Now he was playing cat and mouse with the other one.

He'd seen the movie twice before but this one was a real hell-raiser so he settled back and popped the top of the beercan and watched while Hauer, protector of innocence, stepped out of the tall waving wheat.

He was blind but he could see it all.

The phone rang.

'You're off duty, Covitski. So am I. What are we, going steady or something, you're calling me?'

'You're testy, Rule. You know what testy means? Too much testosterone. Makes you aggressive. You're getting aggressive in your old age. You're getting little white hairs growing out of your ears. What you need to do now is go grab a pair of tweezers. Get rid of those little white hairs. You're gonna want to hear this.'

'You're sure about that?'

'The coroner's office called.'

'No way. They're finished already?'

'Nah. Not till tomorrow. Point is they got something. Wanted to let us have it right away, maybe let us spin with it awhile.'

'They got what?'

'They got teeth marks.'

'*Teeth* marks?'

'Right. Guess where.'

'Jesus, Covitski. His butt. His jugular. His earlobe. How the hell do I know?'

'His *knuckles*.'

Rule let that one sink in.

'Fresh?'

'Uh-huh. Imprint of two front uppers and an incisor across the index and middle finger of his right hand. Our boy Howard gave somebody a knuckle sandwich right before he bought the farm. Now all we got to do is find a few teeth.'

'Any call-in from the wife?'

'Not that I'm aware of. You figure we're looking for the boyfriend. Edwards. That was my idea too.'

'We need to know if anybody's heard from her.'

'I'll phone the station and get right back to you.'

'Make it quick. If she hasn't called I'm going to want to ride out there again.'

'You feel like some company?'

'Sure.'

It sort of surprised him. Covitski had a wife and son. But who could say, maybe he got lonely too.

'Five minutes,' said Covitski.

He decided against the rest of the second beer. He looked in his address book and dialed the number he had for Carole Gardner. On the television they were getting to the part where Hauer slices off the bad guy's eyebrows. 'I also do circumcisions,' he says. Rule was probably going to miss that part. But the nice thing about Cinemax was that unlike life you got plenty of opportunity to catch up with what you missed.

Nobody answered at the Gardner place. He sat and watched and waited by the phone.

Four minutes later he rang again.

Three minutes after that the house was lifeless, empty, dark, and Rule was out working, putting in overtime, about the only thing he had going these days, even the television silent. Hauer on the airwaves avenging something, and nobody there to listen.

Eighteen

Wayne was resourceful. You had to give him that.

Lee considered his resourcefulness sitting alone and uncomfortable on the floor under the motel sink, gagged, his mouth stuffed with white cotton gauze pads and taped shut, his feet bound together behind him and strapped to his thighs so he couldn't straighten his legs and start kicking at the wall, his wrists cuffed to the pipes.

Wayne hadn't even unplugged the phone between the beds.

Why bother?

Lee wasn't going anywhere.

He couldn't even make much of a racket under here, though he was doing his best, slapping the handcuffs against the metal pipes and up against the sink. Trying to shout into the spit-slimy gauze pads – but what came out were only hoarse muffled moans.

It wasn't much.

It was also taking up a hell of a lot of energy. He'd thrash around and then he'd have to stop for a while. He'd listen, hoping that the walls were thin.

They weren't. Either that or next door there was nobody home.

He'd catch his breath and start again. It was all he could do. He could see the .357 magnum on the dresser not ten feet away. It taunted him.

He was scared. The guy was crazy but his act was tight.

Like these handcuffs.

Every time he slammed the pipes or the sink they cut in deeper, scraped off more of his skin. Wayne would take one look at them and know what he'd been up to. The question was would he even give a damn? Or had he reckoned on this too, knowing Lee would try, knowing it would do him no good?

Where were they?

And what did he want with Carole?

With *Carole alone*.

There was no way he was going to find out until Wayne wanted him to. Or unless he somehow got himself free here.

He thrashed. Groaned. He tried to pull the fucking pipe out of the wall but it was no good, he had no leverage. He pounded his head against the bowl of the sink. A series of dull hard-melon thuds.

The headache followed shortly.

To hell with it. He kept pounding.

Rattling his chains.

Jesus! The *audacity*! thought Carole.

They were sitting at a table at the motel bar, a young couple drinking cocktails directly across from them – Irish, she thought, the girl pale and delicate, the man with the eyes of a drinker, ruddy-faced. Two older white-haired men with beers over in the corner. A half-dozen younger men and two women at the bar. A skinny young bartender. A blonde middle-aged cocktail waitress who looked bone-tired of this kind of work, smiling bravely and heavy on her feet.

She could yell out to any and all of them right now. She could dive for the floor.

Help! He's got a gun!

She could get away from him.

If they reacted fast enough.

If they cared to help her. If Wayne didn't kill her before somebody could get the gun away if they wanted to get the gun away, if they tried.

It was at least a possibility.

You first. I'll shoot you first, he'd told her in the parking lot.

Unfortunately she believed him.

She'd already seen that what he said was true. He was a very good shot.

She thought, Look at the chance he's taking, though.

Why?

Is he *that* crazy? Does he want to get caught?

She'd read about people like that, people who committed crimes and then seemed to dare the police to catch up with them, who seemed to like the game almost as much as the crimes themselves. Jack the Ripper sending a kidney to Scotland Yard. Bonnie and Clyde sending photos to the feds and poems to the newspapers.

Egomaniacal crazies.

You can't catch me.

Was that it? Was that why they were sitting here?

Was he daring *her to scream, to try to get away?* She was tempted to call his hand.

She looked around the room.

Who would help?

She couldn't trust them. She couldn't trust any of them to care enough or be good enough even if they did care.

With a shock of recognition she realized that the couple across from them were in the process of breaking up, of ending their relationship. She didn't know why she should notice that but she did.

She could see it plainly on the young woman's face, in the way she was looking at him – it was clear as day – that look of loving him mixed with sadness and longing, with disappointment as she watched him, facing him while he was facing away, watching him closely without him knowing or probably even caring through the long terrible silence between them, the woman's face drawn and pale and plain and then suddenly pretty as she leaned forward saying something light to him, trying to cheer him up. His response intense at first. Angry. Then lethargic, looking away again, showing her that whatever it was, it didn't matter.

It was not just a fight they were having.

It was over.

She saw that they wore no rings.

They'd been dating, then. For how long it was impossible to know. And now it was finished for him – but not for her. She was sitting in this bar, loving him beyond all reason and all hope. She could see the sadness in the mouth, the tenderness in the eyes.

It was painful to watch. She could barely look away.

'Tell me about it,' Wayne said.

He was sipping ice tea through a straw, dunking a wedge of lemon. I hardly ever drink, he'd told her. Proud of that. As though the double scotch she was holding were a great disappointment to him.

Him with the jacket draped over his legs. The gun in his hand beneath it.

A man with a gun. Yet another one.

'I'm sorry. What'd you say?'

'I'd like to hear more about it. I mean for instance, what was it that Howard did that pushed you and Lee over the edge, so to speak? That made you want to kill him? I mean, it must have been something.'

Grinning at her.

'It's none of your business, Wayne.'

'Sure it is. We're in this together, remember?'

'Howard's my business. Our business. Mine and Lee's. Not yours.'

The grin disappeared. He frowned and shook his head.

'Carole. You'd do better to humor me, you know?'

'Why should I humor you, Wayne?'

'I can think of any number of reasons. There's a man in room 233 for one thing. I could slit his throat in a second, couldn't I? Gurgle gurgle. There's a leak under the sink.'

'Fuck you, Wayne.'

But he had her, she knew it. It was nothing new. He'd had her since the moment he'd stepped toward her in the driveway.

Christ! Did she really have to do this? With *him*?

The thought repulsed her.

She'd half expected to have to go over it all someday with the police. She'd almost told Rule the night it had happened. And she'd often wished for a friend apart from Lee good enough and close enough to tell everything to, every miserable detail. But Howard had isolated her by then. There were no good friends anymore. Only business associates and acquaintances and shadows from her past who had drifted away to one part of the country or another.

Her sister and she had long since stopped talking. There were too many memories.

There was no one.

Until now. Until this *parody*.

Their brand-new buddy.

She was damned if she'd give it all up to him. Enough to shut him up. But not all of it.

'He tied me,' she said. 'He raped me. And he cut me.'

'With a knife.'

'Yes, with a knife.'

'That's all?'

She looked at him.

The fucking soulless zombie.

Amazing. That they really existed. Walked, talked, brushed their teeth and went to the toilet just like all the rest of us.

'It was enough, Wayne. Believe me.'

'Where did he cut you?'

'What's the difference?'

'The difference is I want to know. He tied you to what, to the bed?'

'Yes, to the bed.'

'Face-up or face-down?'

'Face-up, for Godsakes!'

'And then he raped you.'

'Yes.'

He was listening intently.

'What did he say?'

'Say?'

'Yes. What did he say to you?'

'He said he was going to let me live. Something like that. That he could use the knife if he wanted to but that he wasn't going to.'

'And then he did.'

'What? Yes. He did.'

'He lied.'

She saw it all over again, heard every word.

Don't worry, I'm not going to kill you, I'm taking off the gag. I'm not going to kill you this time. The point of the knife drifting slowly, scraping across her skin. Drifting down to her navel, pricking it slightly, into her pubic hair. Brushing back and forth. Laughter. *Maybe I'll shave you.* The knife gliding up again . . .

The horror was back, and with it the deep gut-wrenching humiliation. Now as then, she wanted to cry. Now as then, she didn't.

'Yes, Wayne. He lied,' she said.

Her voice was controlled and quiet. You would have to know her far better than Wayne did to hear what this felt like. Lee would know.

'When he raped you. Did he . . . use anything?'

She almost had to laugh at him. Wayne was a goddamn comedian! 'What? A condom? *Howard?*'

'No. I mean, did he *use* anything . . .'

Suddenly she was furious.

'What are we talking about, Wayne?' she hissed. 'A goddamn Coke bottle? His fist? A gerbil, maybe? He used his *cock*, Wayne. You perverted *asshole!*'

He leaned forward.

'Watch it, Carole,' he said. 'I have my little book right here, you know?' He patted his breast pocket. 'I give you a lot of leeway 'cause I scared you pretty bad back there. But I don't bend over backwards forever. Remember that. I was only asking a question. So he raped you. You were face-up and he used his cock. Then he cut you. Where?'

'You don't need to know that, Wayne. You just *want* to know.'

'That's where you're wrong. I do need to know. I need to know everything.'

'Why?'

'So I can make an informed decision.'

'About what?'

'About . . . all of it.'

'All of *what*, Wayne?'

'*About what to do with you* for Chrissakes!'

And there it was. Finally. Out in the open. All the entrails hanging out to dry.

While Wayne just sauntered on through his little white cloud of oblivion.

'What's wrong with you, Carole? You can see that, can't you? You're not a stupid person.'

'No, Wayne. I'm not.'

'So you know I have to decide. So it's up to you to help me decide. So tell me. What can it matter to you anyhow? It's over and done with. Past is past.'

Howard and Wayne. Under the skin they were so damn similar she felt a hot wave of nausea just being in his presence. *Past is past. Over and done with.*

Hey! Why can't you just forget all about it, bitch?

She could still hear Howard yelling something very much like that out on her lawn that night. *What the hell's wrong with you?*

When the past was not remotely past. Not when it included the shame and pain she could feel to this day. Not when she could still feel the blade of the knife – not its tip this time, no, its *blade* – slide across her breast to the fear-erect nipple, feel it slice ever so slightly across the nipple's flat wide tip and then continue, the pressure harder now, a thin red line burgeoning wet across the valley between her breasts, as Howard's pleasure bloomed inside her, she could feel it obscenely big between her legs and then jerking, spurting as the blade crossed to the right breast, the other nipple, biting deeper, bisecting the soft ridge of flesh as she screamed and screamed into the friendless still night.

Wayne and Howard. Howard and Wayne.

'I could make you strip, you know. I could take you back to the motel and *make* you show me. Instead, I'm asking you.'

How they do love power, she thought. How they gloried in it.

'Yes, you could, Wayne. But you wouldn't see anything if you did,' she lied. She lit a cigarette.

'He cut me practically everywhere, if you have to know. Shoulders, belly, breasts, thighs. Very small nicks. Nothing serious. They healed. But they were enough, don't you think?' She exhaled. 'It took him quite a while.'

That much, anyway, was true.

Wayne was studying her, nodding. It looked to Carole as though he was going to believe her.

'Yes,' he said. 'It's enough.' Then he laughed. 'Enough for *me*, anyway.' He patted his book again. *All the names in there. All the offenses.*

'But is it enough for you? I wonder.'

He studied her a while longer. Then sipped his tea and shrugged. 'Sure. Sure it is. I guess it's plenty.' He smiled. 'Don't worry. I won't make you show me. I honestly think I know how humiliating that would be for you.'

She wanted to laugh in his face. The sanctimonious little prick.

Humiliation – real humiliation — was not even in his vocabulary.

To her it was an enemy so old it had almost, once, become a friend.

'Okay. You told me,' he said. 'I'm glad. There's something I want you to do for me now.' He looked around the bar.

'You know, I've been dreaming of sitting here doing this since the first night I saw you and Lee in the restaurant. Us sitting talking like this. Us with our little secret.'

She sipped her scotch. She felt out of the woods for the moment. She would show him nothing.

'What?' she said.

'Hmmm?'

'You said there was something you wanted me to do for you. What?'

'Oh, right. I was distracted. You're very beautiful, you know that?'

She let it pass.

'You see those two?' he said.

He nodded toward the couple across from them. The Irish woman and her boyfriend.

The silence between them hadn't broken. The woman was gazing down into her lap now, gazing at her fingers. Lightly clenching and unclenching them. *So much pain*, Carole thought. The man was still sitting to one side facing away from her, his legs crossed, casually smoking a cigarette. Their parting so inconsequential to him.

'What about them?'

'I want you to go over. Ask for a smoke or something. Get them to talk to you. Get them over here to the table.'

He slurped at the ice and the dregs of his tea through the bent straw. His eyes skittered.

So that she saw, long before she heard, what he had in mind.

'No,' she said.

She had to pre-empt him. To draw the line. To stop this freezing feeling suddenly clutching at her insides.

Not them. Never. Not this poor sad lonely girl.

I'd kill myself first.

But it was as though he hadn't heard her. And she knew then that she was not out of the woods here by a long shot. She had never been, not for a second. Telling him what he'd wanted to hear had meant nothing. A minor test of obedience. And fear.

Good doggie.

His voice was cold and hollow.

'I want them,' he said. 'And you are going to get them for me. So finish your scotch. Finish your cigarette.

'And go over.'

Nineteen

The visit was illegal, strictly informational. He hoped Covitski was being neat about it downstairs. Ideally it should look like nobody had been here at all.

So far there wasn't much anyway. Prescription downers in the medicine cabinet. Men's clothes in the drawers and closet in two distinct sizes – they'd be Lee's and Howard's. So she was slow getting rid of his clothing. So what.

Then he opened the drawer to the night-table.

And *this* was interesting.

He walked downstairs. Covitski was standing in the living room.

'What's wrong with this picture?' he said.

Rule scanned the room.

'Clipboard,' he said.

'You got it.'

He walked over. The clipboard looked out of place on the polished glass table. It was the only thing sitting there. There were three sheets of unused lined yellow paper clipped to it, and on top of it, a yellow number two pencil. He focused on the pencil. Covitski was looking at it too.

'Either of them strike you as the kind who chews his pencils?' Covitski asked him.

'No. In fact I can't even figure the clipboard. You could say she maybe uses the board, jotting down specs on houses, land measurements, that kind of thing. Okay. But only three sheets of paper? Just three? She'd have a whole pad there or else the remains of one. Plus there's no writing.'

'His, maybe. Edwards'.'

'Same problem. Plus it'd be in the briefcase, wouldn't it?' The briefcase was still standing in the middle of the room. Definitely a man's. Thick, bulky, and showing wear. A woman would pick something lighter, narrower. And she'd probably take care of it better. Nobody had touched it, apparently, since he'd noticed it through the window.

'So we got us a third party,' said Covitski. 'Hired gun?'

'Could be.'

It was possible. He wondered if Lee and Carole would be stupid enough or desperate enough to involve somebody else in their killing. If they had done the killing in the first place. He guessed that smarter people had done dumber things.

Twenty-one years ago you had Watergate.

'I don't suppose you came across a .357 magnum,' he said.

Covitski looked surprised. He shook his head.

'Hell, no.'

'There's a box of shells in a drawer up there, maybe a dozen rounds missing. But no weapon.'

'You tossed the room?'

Rule nodded.

'There's nothing down here. I been everywhere. She'd probably keep it up there anyway, wouldn't she? With the cartridges.'

'Probably. You know what?' he said. 'I keep thinking about the highway. Your shooting. The red Volvo. The guy's description of the male and female.'

'What, you figure they've gone loony or something? Out on the highway shooting up the populace? Hell, Joe, I can see them doing Howard but . . .' He shook his head again.

'Anyhow, a .38 did that one. Not a magnum. You really think there's a connection?'

'I don't know what to think. You found nothing at all in the kitchen?'

'Nope.'

'She was taking prescription downers. The bottle's half-empty. Dated less than a week ago, so she was popping quite a few of them. It might indicate problems.'

'Unless Edwards was taking them too.'

'Possible.'

Two cats, one black and one tabby, were sitting in the middle of the room about three feet apart looking back and forth from Rule to Covitski. Studying them. Like, *are these guys friends or enemies*? The black one was Beast. He forgot the name of the tabby.

He sighed. 'I'll tell you, the thing that bothers me, that brings me back to the Volvo, is the two cars parked out front. That and the clipboard. They both say visitor to me. If they're not home, there has to be a third car somewhere. With them in it.

'We'll check the cab companies. But it's unlikely they'd have problems with two cars on the same day. My guess is that we'll find that nobody picked up anybody at this address. Not today.

'So then we're looking for a third car. Probably with three people in it. So why not the Volvo? I mean, how often does it happen that this town gets two homicides in less than a week?'

Covitski shrugged. 'Never.'

The last violent death – if it even qualified as violent death – that Rule had seen was over three months ago. A guy had swallowed his dentures. He was a tourist from New Jersey whose wife had read him a wrong turn on the map. The guy threw such a fit about it that he'd simply inhaled the dentures. They'd thought it was a heart attack all the way to the autopsy.

'I think we should go scc how the computer's moving on that plate ID. Also if we can get handgun registrations for Gardner or Edwards.'

'Aw hell, Joe. It's damn near ten. Mae's gonna kill me.'

'I'll drop you off. No problem.'

They headed for the door.

'Did she feed the cats?'

'Huh?'

'In the kitchen. Did the cats have food and water?'

'I dunno.'

Rule turned and walked back into the kitchen. Covitski followed. There was a half inch of water in the bottom of a white glass bowl. The food dishes were empty. Like most cats these two were sloppy eaters. The remains of their last meal were scattered all over the floor. The food was old and crusted. Probably the morning feeding. There were pop-top cans of Friskies on the counter.

He opened one.

'I thought we weren't supposed to be here,' said Covitski.

'The cats won't tell.'

They were rubbing at his ankles now, the tabby giving him her backside and the black the side of her mouth where the scent-glands were located.

He split the can between them.

The cats dug in.

'She should have fed them,' he said. 'You got the cars, you got the clipboard, you got the cats. Something's wrong.'

They walked to the door.

'You still want me to drop you?' he asked.

'Nah. The hell with it,' said Covitski. 'Maybe tomorrow I'll get a life. Maybe Mae won't axe me. I read somewhere that women find men who are dedicated to their professions very sexy.'

Rule laughed. 'I wouldn't know.'

'I mean, you got to figure Albert Schweitzer got some, don't you?'

'I suppose you do.'

Covitski came back from the men's room drying his hands on a paper towel. Rule was at the computer.

'We got it,' he said.

Covitski leaned over his shoulder and read aloud. Rule took a pad and started writing.

"'Red '93 Volvo, Vermont State driver's license number G02333J6, registered to Wayne Philip Lock, 4183 Gastonboro Road, Barstow." Jesus, look at this! They pulled the guy's license on a DWI!'

'Get on the phone to the State Police. Tell them we need an APB, possibly armed and dangerous. Give them the DWI case number. One to three occupants of the vehicle. Give them descriptions of Lee Edwards and Carole Gardner. Meantime I'm going to punch in a request for handgun IDs on Edwards, Gardner, and this joker. Okay?'

'Okay.'

He had a pretty good feeling on this. It was why he loved the job those times he didn't hate the job. It was why he put in the hours and took the suits to the cleaners and shaved every morning and maybe why Ann was gone.

He figured that in every cut of meat there was something spoiling.

He looked at Covitski.

'Would you want to bet that somebody here owns a. 38?' he said.

Somebody did.

By ten-forty-five a smart, ambitious, and very easy-to-look-at lady named Pamela Donelly who was the Assistant DA on call that night was working on a search warrant, the auto ID and the .38 constituting to her mind sufficient probable cause, and they were back in the car headed for Wayne Lock's home on Gastonboro Road.

Covitski drove. Rule sat on the passenger side watching for the Volvo even though he knew the chances were ridiculously slim that Lock would still be in the area. Sometimes you got lucky.

The road was narrow, winding, nearly empty of traffic at this hour. Lock lived in the old part of town bordering Woolcott, the houses set close together, built mostly after World War II and built badly for the most part so that half of them had begun to lean as they settled, an inch or two this way or that way, and it gave them a slightly drunken look that the sparse starving shade trees curbside didn't much enhance.

It was an ugly, gnarled neighborhood surrounded by mountains, rolling hills and beautiful farmland. An insult to all that, a gob of spit in the tourist's eye. Nothing graceful or even interesting anywhere.

Until you got to Fort Ticonderoga here.

The fence began along the cracked sidewalk, turned an asymmetrical corner on each side along the driveway and the neighboring yard and then marched down the lawn like an invading army of white birch pickets stabbing massively at the thin pitiful grass. The numbers *4183* looked to have been burned into the birchwood of the hinged door with a soldering iron and then colored in with bootblack. The pickets looked to Rule to be ten feet tall.

On the left-hand side in front, one of them was missing. A gap in Lock's wooden suit of armor. Other than that the thing looked impregnable. Of course that was just an illusion, all you had to do was open this swinging hinged door here and . . .

. . . hope to hell that he wasn't waiting with the .38 on the other side. He wasn't.

They walked to the door and knocked. The house was dark inside, the blinds pulled. He knocked again. Nothing. The driveway had been empty when they came in. No Volvo.

Somewhere a dog was barking.

The search warrant wouldn't arrive for another couple of hours yet. For the moment they were stuck here.

'What do you want to do?' said Covitski.

'Let's go talk to the neighbors, see if one of them spoke to him today, maybe saw him drive on out of here. Maybe knew where he was going.'

The house with the dog was easy to find – it was right next door past some hedges, and the dog was still yapping. Its owner was a six-foot unshaven sixty-year-old hulk of a man with a belly pouring over his dirty brown slacks and straining the thin white T-shirt. He stood on his ragged wooden porch plucking at his red suspenders.

The dog was on a leash by his side. The dog was pacing passionately.

Rule was glad of the leash. The dog looked to be half mastiff and half rhino and didn't seem too thrilled to have them there.

'You want Lock?' the man said.

'That's right,' Rule said. He opened his wallet and showed the man his badge.

He didn't even glance at it. His face broke open into a big wet grin.

It was not a pretty thing to see.

'It's Wayne Lock you're looking for?' he said.

'Yes, sir. That's correct.'

His smile got even broader. He laughed and shook his head and plucked at the suspenders.

'Son,' he said, 'in that case ol' Happy here and I are gonna have to invite you in.'

Twenty

Lock was raging.

Lee'd seen it from the moment he pushed her through the door, then stomped over and ripped the tape off his face. He spit out the cotton pads.

She was sitting on the bed now, rigid, her hands gripped tight together and staring at Wayne while he paced back and forth from door to sink, slamming at the sink with his fist, turning and kicking the chest of drawers, turning again toward Lee. Gazing wildly back at her reflected image in the mirror but never at her directly, only through the mirror. And apart from ripping off the tape, never seeming to notice Lee down there at all.

He could smell the sour stink of the man.

Something unravelling.

'I ask you *one thing*, Carole! One fucking little thing. One miserable little favor, but no. *Oh no!*

'What? Are you too *moral* for me, Carole? To help me out here? Are you *better* than me?

'You think you are *better* than me?

'I don't know what in the hell to do with you. I don't know what to do! I have given you a lot of fucking slack, Carole, you know? A lot of fucking slack. Because I liked you. Because I wanted to help you. But I'm telling you, you are on the top of my shit-list now, baby! You are at the fucking *pinnacle*!

'You *bitch*!'

Lee watched the words slam into her like body-blows. There wasn't much he could think to do to deflect them. But then he saw Wayne turn, walking toward her, finally looking at her directly with his hand going to his back pocket where the gun was and he knew he had to try.

'Wayne.'

Softly. Go easy now.

'Wayne. What's the problem? Maybe I can help here.'

He whirled. Walked over and kicked the pipes just below his hands.

'Your *bitch*! Your bitch is the fucking problem!'

'Whatever it is, Wayne, we can deal with it.'

'Oh really? *Deal with this!*'

He saw the kick coming and had time to move his head but not enough time. He smelled dirt and shoeleather and felt the sharp crack at the back of his neck that sent his forehead smashing against the pipe. Looked up and saw Wayne's face, the grim thin set to the mouth, lips pulled down and back almost comically thin and wide, a parody of somebody's little-boy pout except that the eyes were furious and crazy and the foot was coming up again.

He threw himself to the side.

The foot thudded against the sink.

'You *fucker*!'

Then Carole was up off the bed shouting *Leave him alone* and coming towards them – no, *going for the magnum on the dresser*! – just as the foot was drawing back again and Wayne saw her in the mirror, righted himself, turned, took one step toward her and she walked right into the blow, right into his fist. It took her low in the stomach. It doubled her over and sunk her to her knees.

And someone was pounding on the wall.

'Hey! You! Enough in there for Chrissake!'

He looked up and Lee thought of some animal abruptly smelling smoke, some distant brushfire. Wayne stood frozen. Poised, silent, scenting the wind and crouched to run. The mad eyes suddenly cunning. Instantly deciding. Snatching the gun off the dresser.

'Not a sound!' he hissed. 'You, move away. Back on the bed. I swear I'll use this. I don't care, you understand me? *I don't care.*'

Carole clutched at her belly and hauled herself up.

He shoved the gun into Lee's face, reached in his pocket and took out a key and held it out to him.

'Here. Just the left wrist. And don't you fuck with me.'

Lee took the key and fumbled it into the keyhole. The cuff snapped open, dangling.

He massaged the red chafing. His skin was torn, raw, burning.

'Untie yourself.'

He worked at the knots. Feet first and then across the legs, the blood pouring into them, making them throb, making him aware of his pulse inside them.

'Okay. Up.'

He stood. His knees were shaky, his right leg still half asleep from being bound up behind him for so long. He had to urinate and the mere fact that he did unmanned him. So that was where he'd come to. Wayne was literally scaring the piss out of him now.

Christ!

'You too.'

She stood up.

'Okay, now out the door,' he said. 'We're checking out.'

He pushed the gun hard into Lee's back and he grunted, the sound forced out of him. The sound was to make sure that Carole knew the gun was there. He pulled open the door. He turned off the light behind them and took the suitcase off the bed and they stepped outside into the warm night air.

They crossed the dimly lit concrete landing. He walked them down the stairs.

The Volvo stood facing them.

'Around back,' he said.

They walked to the rear of the car. Lee scanned the windows of the motel, scanned the doors. The doors were all shut, the windows curtained. No faces peered out. The lot was quiet.

Wayne set the suitcase down and opened the trunk.

'Get in,' he said to Lee, 'you first.'

'Wayne . . . Jesus Christ, Wayne . . . people... *die* in these things!'

He heard the quiver in his voice. He hated the fact that it was there but he couldn't do a damn thing about it and he felt the urge to piss again. He tasted bile in his mouth.

He thought, *That was what fear tasted like*. Bile.

Wayne was smiling.

'Look closely, Lee. I've already taken care of that.'

There were two small holes punched into the lid of the trunk just above the logo.

'God knows I love this car,' said Wayne. 'It was really very unpleasant for me having to make them. But you had to think this through and prepare for all contingencies, and I used the drill so they're neat enough, don't you think? I mean, they hardly show. I'll have to do something eventually about rust, though.

'Actually I expected to be putting somebody else in here. But now I guess it's you.'

He lifted the gun.

'So you do it or you fucking die, Lee. Personally I don't give a shit either way.'

He climbed in, shifted his weight toward the back, curling his legs over the jack beneath him to make room for her and waited for her to climb in. It felt like they were being buried alive in some communal grave, just the two of them. In a grave that smelled of grease and metal and gasoline, and then suddenly the scent of her, the woman-smell. Almost its echo, barely perceptible.

The scent of flowers.

Twenty-one

Susan pulled up across from Wayne's house and saw the car in front and thought, *Okay, now who is this?*

She'd called the bar three times over the course of two hours and he still wasn't there. Mikey, the floor manager, made it clear to her that a fourth call wouldn't be necessary. That if he came in now he could just go the hell back home again.

She'd called his house half a dozen times and there wasn't any answer. She was worried.

Wayne was responsible. Punctual. She'd tried to tell Mikey that – that if something weren't really wrong with him he'd at least have called in – but Mikey couldn't have cared less. Said he was a piece-of-shit bartender anyway, which wasn't fair, and that he'd already filled his spot with a part-timer who was looking to go full-time and that was that. Told her to call the cops if she was so damn worried.

She hadn't called the police – she wasn't family, after all. Or married to him or anything.

But she *had* decided to drive over.

And now here was this strange car in front and . . .

. . . two strange men walking toward her from the Roberts' house next door.

She rolled up the driver's side window.

The taller of the two men bent down and looked at her through the window and smiled. She wasn't reassured.

Not until he opened his wallet and showed her the badge inside.

And then she was reassured and scared at the same time.

She rolled down the window.

'Y . . . yes?'

The man was still smiling.

'I'm Lieutenant Rule and this is Lieutenant Covitski. May I ask for some ID, please?'

She got her wallet out of her purse and handed him her driver's license. The man angled it up so he could read it in the moonlight – the streetlight was out again, just like hers was going – and then handed it back to her.

'Do you know the gentleman living at this address? Wayne Lock? Are you a friend of his, Miss Olsen?'

She felt herself blushing. She looked away.

'I . . . guess you could say I used to be his girlfriend.'

'Not any more?'

'We had a kind of fight.'

'A fight?'

'A disagreement.'

'Have you seen him at all today?'

She shook her head. 'Not since Saturday.'

'Talk to him?'

'No.'

'Not since Saturday?'

'No.'

He looked at her. Studied her. For some reason the way he was looking at her made her feel guilty. She hadn't done anything.

'Why are you here, then?' he said.

His voice wasn't unkind, she thought. Just curious. 'I was worried about him. He works tonight. He's a bartender over at the Black Locust Tavern. And he hasn't shown up or called in and that's not like Wayne.'

'I see. So you drove over.'

'Yes.'

'Any idea where he might be?'

'God, I don't know.'

She thought that there really wasn't anyplace in particular. And anyplace was possible. She really did want to help the man. She wanted to ask him what was wrong and why they were looking for Wayne but she couldn't quite bring herself to do that. She didn't know why but she couldn't.

And then it was like he read her mind.

'We're going to want to talk with you about a few things, Susan. All right? And I'm sure you have questions too. But right now I want you to think. It's very, very important. Can you come up with anyplace he might go? If he were in trouble or had some sort of problem maybe?'

'Problem?'

'Uh-huh.'

She thought about it. There just *wasn't* anywhere.

If he had a problem he'd have come to her, wouldn't he? Even after . . . what had happened.

'I know it's late,' said the man, 'but might he have gone to see his mother?'

'His *mother*?'

114

'Yes.'

'What do you mean? His mother's dead.'

And for a moment the man just looked at her. She thought that his eyes were very nice, very pretty for a policeman's eyes and sort of sad-looking. Sort of lonely.

'According to his neighbor over there,' the man said quietly, 'Wayne's mother is a quarter of a mile away, at Sweetwood Retirement Home over on Barstow Road. He said she's been there for about three years now. I guess Wayne didn't tell you. Sorry.'

And she realized, then, why the eyes were sad. And just who it was he was sad for.

Twenty-two

The nurse was not pleased at all.

She was a redhead in her early thirties and unmarried – no ring – and Rule would have liked to have made her much happier, but that was not going to happen. He regretted this as he watched her long lovely legs move ahead of them down the oak panelled hall past the sunny painted landscapes on the walls and the hard institutional chairs placed just outside the rooms.

He regretted it deeply.

Dorothy Lock's room was the last one over on the right, she said. From here you could see into what the nurse had told him was the library. To Rule it looked more like a mid-price hotel lobby than a library, with more oak panelling, more bright vistas on the walls, plush imitation-leather easy chairs and sofas and only a smattering of books on the shelves. Mostly paperbacks.

At this hour, of course, the library was empty.

The nurse had made it very clear that lights-out was ten o'clock sharp.

And here it was past eleven-thirty.

She opened the door and turned on the overhead lights. The room was wallpapered, a pretty light floral print design. There was an easy chair, an inexpensive dresser with a mirror, a writing desk with a spindle chair, an overhead tv mounted on the wall facing the bed, one small window with a screen, a rotary-dial wall-phone, a bathroom and a single closet.

The dresser and desktop were bare.

No books. No pictures. No perfume bottles.

Nothing.

Rule could get no sense of habitation. Whatever the woman owned, whatever possessions might indicate her personality or identity were somewhere tucked away.

She was facing the window, a tiny huddled body covered by a sheet.

The nurse walked over and touched her lightly on the shoulder, then drew back instantly. As though touching a hot stove or something charged with current.

'Mrs Lock.'

116

He realized then that the nurse was not just annoyed with them because of the hour.

It was this particular patient or resident or whatever you called them. Something about the woman bothered her.

Something about the woman *scared* her.

He began to see why. The old woman turned so abruptly it was almost shocking. Suddenly wide awake, her milky blue eyes took in Rule and Covitski at a glance.

He had the sense of being swallowed.

The nurse took one step back. The woman ignored her and swung her legs off the bed. The legs were thin and naked, webbed with ropy blue veins, the skin dry and cracked as the dry bed of a stream.

Her lips were thin. They pulled back in a sly smile that looked surprisingly glad to see them.

'You're police,' she said. Her voice was low. It seemed much younger than the rest of her. Her long grey stringy hair had billowed out in sleep.

'Yes, ma'am,' said Rule. 'My name's Rule and this is Lieutenant Covitski. We understand from Miss . . .'

'Maitland,' said the nurse.

'. . . Miss Maitland, that you had a call tonight. We're wondering if it might have been from Wayne, your son.'

'My son?'

'Excuse me,' said the nurse. 'If you don't need me any more . . .'

She was already moving past them through the door. To Rule it seemed like a getaway. A whiff of spicy perfume elbowed its way past the fusty old-woman smell in the room.

'That's fine. Thanks,' he said.

She closed the door behind her.

The woman was watching him.

'What about my son?'

'We need to ask him some questions, ma'am.'

Her eyes narrowed. He noticed that the flesh around the eyes was deeply lined. The lines ran all the way down through the hollow depressions of her cheeks. Her mouth on the other hand was almost without them and none of the lines were deep. As though the accustomed expression of the mouth was no expression at all.

He felt Covitski shift uneasily beside him.

'My son,' she said.

Her low voice filled the room completely, hung there, as though the room were empty of all furnishings, even of life.

She was staring straight into his eyes. He had to resist the impulse to look away.

'You want to know if he called me.'

'Yes.'

'Today.'

'That's correct.'

She leaned forward on the bed.

'My son is a cunting little coward,' she said. 'Did you know that?'

The voice was as empty, flat and desolate as her dressertop. Despite the words he did not sense hatred there. He sensed no emotion at all. Only statement of fact. Her son was a cunting little coward. End of story.

He wanted out. He needed some fresh air.

The nurse was right.

This one was better left asleep.

'Do you know what I suffer from?' she said. 'Fainting spells. That's right. They happen sometimes once a week, sometimes twice a day. It's my blood pressure. Otherwise my health is perfect. I get fainting spells. And they are what have allowed my son Wayne to gain custodianship over me and put me into this place so that I can smell the shit of the dying all day. My son cannot take care of me in the home I lived in for thirty-five years, he says, he has to go to work and is afraid to leave me alone, he says. Do you know what the shit of the dying smells like, Officer Rule? I doubt that you do.'

Rule glanced at Covitski. He saw he was not alone in wanting out of there. Covitski couldn't have looked worse if it were his own mother sitting in front of him talking this way.

There was poison in the room and it was lethal. Quietly leaking out of the empty walls and closet. Leaking out of the bed. It all belonged to her.

Poison was what she owned.

It filled the empty room.

'Old onions,' she said. 'The shit of the dying smells like old rotten onions. There is shit in the halls even as we speak. Did you know that? There is shit in the sink. They have to diaper them here but it doesn't help. They empty it into the sinks, into the toilets. They walk in it through the halls. No, my little baby boy did not call me tonight. The call I received was from an old admirer. Who is dead now. I have many who are dead.'

Poison. Madness.

Wayne had lived with this.

Covitski touched his sleeve.

He was right. They weren't going to gain anything more here tonight than what they'd already gotten. Which was plenty. It didn't excuse Lock but it went a distance toward explaining him.

'If he were in trouble, where would he go?' he asked.

The question was pro forma at this point but you never knew.

'I have no idea,' she said.

'And when was the last time you saw him?'

The woman smiled. The bed began to shake.

He realized she was laughing.

It was soundless, eerie.

She stopped. Her face went dreamy.

'When I had him in my mouth,' she said.

And then she was lost, remembering.

'Three years ago. July or maybe August. It was a very warm day. I made him come. I always do. I had him in my mouth and I swallowed. I sucked him dry.'

She laughed. The laugh of an evil sly young girl.

And God help him, he believed her.

Twenty-three

He was a bee. The world was his flower.

He was pollinating the world, carrying the seeds of life with him in the broad wide circle of his flight, dropping the seeds into the ground where they would roil and decay and finally burst open, their flowering the turbulence of maggots, the birth of flies, the endless chain of life.

Route 89 South to 2 North to 93 South at St Johnsbury, down through the White Mountains, in New Hampshire again, down through the National Forest, dark empty highway, barely a car on the road, trees looming. He could hear Carole and Lee bumping around in back when the roads got rougher. They could die in there or not. Like everybody else all they wanted was to hurt him. It wasn't going to happen. His book was filling up with them. He could feel it press against his chest, weighty, massive.

Down through Compton and Blair and Livermore Falls to 3A and Plymouth, cruising south through the late-night dimly lit college town, yet another fucking college town, passing the Trolley Car Restaurant twice and passing yet again, nobody on the streets but a stumbling drunk old man. Not enough. Not good enough.

Driving.

North on Route 3, *buzzing*, a long steep road sliding gently down into an open valley and up again, the occasional house, lights on in the window, forest on all sides and then a left at Avery's General Store, dark, deserted at this hour and driving the winding mountain road to Ellsworth, past the Chapel of St John of the Mountains bone-white in the moonlight, perched old and tiny like a skeleton on the side of a hill, Rev Roger Pecke Cleveland, Minister. Onto a narrow dirt road, climbing.

This was going nowhere.

Turning, kicking up dust – he could taste it in his mouth, feel it in his teeth.

How you doing back there? He could feel them bumping around pretty good now.

Back down the road past a small country graveyard, a beaver pond, over a bridge, back to 3A, back toward Plymouth and State College.

120

He was about a mile and a half from town when he saw them in the valley by the side of the road.

And oh, he was young. Oh, she was pretty.

He pulled over.

It was farmland all around here. A wide open field down below. A barn and a silo. Deserted.

He reached into the back seat. Into the open suitcase.

This made up for so much.

The boredom. The endless days of being and yet . . . *not being.* The unfairness of all the people around him. The traps first his father and then, later, his mother had set for him.

This was what he was meant to do. To be.

The night wrapped him in rich destiny and its cloak was soft and warm. 'Need a hand?' he said.

The girl was standing over the boy with one small thin blue-veined naked hand on her hip and the other resting on the roof of the car. She looked up and smiled as he got out and slammed the door. The girl was wearing cutoff jeans and a white tailored shirt many sizes too big for her rolled up at the sleeves. The girl was trusting.

The boy glanced over his shoulder. He was working on the lugs with the lug wrench. The boy smiled too.

'Thanks, but we're fine,' he said.

The boy had done this before. He was competent.

We're fine.

'Not really,' said Wayne, and produced the gun.

Lynn Naylor had considered her luck debatable.

At the age of ten she was riding her cousin's bike down a neighbor's driveway. The driveway was newly paved – it looked smooth and inviting.

The bike was much too small for her. In fact they'd only recently taken off its training wheels. And it didn't have hand-brakes. Only foot-brakes. And her legs were so long it was hard for her to get the proper leverage.

So that when the driveway wound around the back of the house and plunged suddenly down a long steep hill she couldn't stop. She couldn't get the leverage. She dragged her bare feet along the fresh macadam until her toes were bloody but it didn't help.

At the bottom of the hill was a dome-shaped granite boulder over ten feet high at its jagged peak, twenty-two feet long, and she tried to steer toward the narrow space – just a path, really – between the boulder and the thick grove of pines surrounding it.

By the time she reached the bottom the bike was going much too fast for her to manage.

She clipped the edge of the rock at over forty miles an hour, that was what the police had told her. The borrowed bike was a twisted ruin. At the moment of impact she had thrown her arm straight out in front of her. And that had saved her life. Her forearm snapped – she could still remember the sound of it snapping – but it also vaulted her over on top of the rock instead of head-first into it.

She came away with eighteen stitches in her back, ten scarred toes, a mild concussion and a broken arm.

On the one hand she supposed that was pretty lucky.

On the other hand you had to factor in the driveway itself and its particular allure for her on that day. You had to factor in the blind sudden plunge. The too-small bicycle. And the rock.

Not so lucky.

A year ago she and Ben had totaled his Ford. They were driving a rainslick road on a hot summer day and another car – a Pontiac – was passing, its rear tires sliding over no more than a foot or so, just enough so that the rear of the Pontiac kissed their left front bumper and sent them flying off the road over an embankment. The next thing she remembered she was sitting inside the roof of the car and Ben was already coming around the other side, opening the door and pulling her out.

They emerged without a scratch.

But in this as in the other incident her luck had to be considered debatable. You had the fact that she had lived through it at all balanced by the fact that it had happened in the first place, and for her the two seemed to cancel each other out. The coin had flipped – and amazingly, had twice now landed on its edge. It proved nothing to her except that, against the wildest odds, she was still alive.

Ben Stillman *knew* he was fortunate. No question.

His proof was simple.

He had college, he had work, he had a future, and he had Lynn. Not necessarily in that order.

College had been hard to come by because it was hard to afford. His father was a Patterson, New Jersey stonemason, union all the way, and when the union said sorry, you don't work his father didn't work. Which was often. But Ben had held down his own jobs since he was fifteen. He'd saved and he'd studied. His mom worked as an office clerk and that had helped some too. But mostly he was making it on his own. He made sure his grades were fine in high school and now here he was with a working scholarship to Plymouth State, well on his way to a Masters in Business at an even better school two years down the line.

He was not going to be some union man. He was not going to work with

122

his hands when he did work and drink and sit in front of the tube all day when he didn't. He would not grow a gut. He *would* have money.

Then there was Lynn.

Back in Patterson a girl like Lynn would never have looked at him. He wasn't even sure they *had* girls like Lynn in Patterson. She was subtle, funny, educated – private schools, mostly. With one year in public school 'for seasoning.' She was lovely as any woman he'd ever met and she was probably going to be wealthy one day in her own right. Her family had old Boston money. She'd been lazy grade-wise through high school but she wasn't anymore, not since meeting him, she was going after her own Masters and they were looking at the same schools together – Stanford, Wharton, Harvard – the top of the line all the way.

In bed she was responsive fire. Heart and brains. Controlled and measured unpredictability.

He felt that there was nothing he wanted that he either did not already have or could not someday reach.

There would be children. Vacations. Leisure.

Between them they could do anything.

They could even change a tire.

So he didn't need this guy in the slightest but thought it was nice of him to offer. It was the sort of thing he liked about New Hampshire. People were really neighborly. It was too bad a person couldn't generate much money living here. For that you needed cities. New York or L.A. or Washington.

But you could certainly consider retiring here some day. Homes could be had for a song and taxes were among the lowest in the nation.

It almost amazed him. That here he was as *young* as he was looking that far down the road.

So that when this fellow *crossed* the road he didn't give him a thought, just kept working on the lugs – and he never saw the gun or the big claw hammer, one in each hand, until the hammer came down on him once and then a second time, and he could hear Lynn screaming into the silent warm void of the night that seemed to trickle down over his forehead, his cheeks, and into his eyes.

Blinding all that vision.

He used his foot to shove the boy's body under the car. The road's grading made it easy. The boy rolled under.

'You know how to use a jack?' he said.

The girl nodded, looking not at him but at the gun.

He liked the way she cried. No sobbing. No sound at all. Just a steady wash of tears.

'Jack it down. Then throw everything into the trunk. Got that?'

123

The girl went to work.

Two cars parked a few feet away from one another on opposite sides of the road, both safely off to the shoulder. Nobody would give them a thought. With the car jacked down you wouldn't see the boy.

Which meant he'd have some time here.

She stared up into moonlight.

The trees were black and grey and maggot white. The man in front of her was black. A silhouette. She could smell the damp earth beneath her, smell the chafed bark of the tree, the sharp hot metallic smell of twisted, abraded wire.

She was lying on her back. Old leaves soft beneath her. A pillow of moss and lichen lumpy beneath her head.

He had wound the length of bailing wire around the slim trunk of the birch tree and then around her wrists, twisting the wire off tight over each wrist with a pair of pliers.

She could taste the thick salt of snot and tears.

She could not stop trembling. It was electric. A low steady hum.

'I think I'll let you live,' he said.

He knelt beside her and lifted off her sandals one by one and set them carefully down behind him. The gun never left his hand. Nor the pliers in the other.

'I'm going to fuck you, though,' he said. 'You understand that?'

She couldn't see his eyes. But his voice was almost mild. She nodded.

'Lift up.'

She raised her hips. The man unzipped her cutoffs and pulled them off her. Folded them once and placed them beside her sandals.

'Lift again.'

Then suddenly the man was a blur of tears.

But she did as she was told.

The leaves, the ground were cold and damp.

He folded the panties and placed them next to the cutoffs. Sandals and clothes in an even line directly behind him.

He unbuttoned her shirt starting with the top button and moving slowly down – and only when he was finished did he part it, revealing her.

'Beautiful,' he whispered.

He leaned closer, black, blotting out the moon and sky. The gun moved to her lips, its barrel cold, parting them. *Please*, she tried to say. It came out *preesss*. The barrel stayed there, pressed against her teeth. She felt the chill of metal, the pliers, circle over the flesh of her breast and then spiral slowly inward, teasing her toward mute horror. She felt them open and

124

embrace the blossoming ridge of flesh. Closing. Gently squeezing. Cold, jagged. Terrible.

Then grasping, lifting.

Her body arched.

'I could use these on you,' said the man.

It was as though he were reciting something he'd learned. As though he'd got it somewhere and the words weren't even his.

He laughed. The jaws released her. *'But I won't,'* he said.

She fell back against the leaves.

He didn't know. He didn't understand.

He already had.

And then later she was wet with him, wet between her legs, breasts slick with his sweat. Smelling of him. Droplets from his forehead sliding down across her cheeks.

He dropped away from her next to the line of clothing and stood and buckled his pants.

She hurt.

He had used his fingernails, his teeth. She hurt everywhere.

'You got to change it,' he said. 'You got to change it every time.' His breath was coming in gasps. He was not strong. She had learned that. Not without the gun. His arms and legs were thin and bony. He did not have too much stamina.

She thought of Ben and pushed the thought away.

Pushed it all away.

He was tucking in his shirt, looking down at her.

'Your *MO*, I mean. You know what that means? That means *modus operandi*. The way you do things. If you don't change it then they catch you.'

She realized that he was talking about her death.

'Which is why I used the hammer. Smart, you see? First they're looking for a .38 and then a .357 and now a hammer. Three different people, right?'

No, she thought. *Four.*

When he leaned over again she noticed that he was still short of breath. Another, shorter length of wire was in his hand. He wound it once around her neck and grasped hold of the ends.

She didn't struggle. There was only one possible way to live through this. There had never been another.

The coin had to come to rest on its spinning edge, neither heads nor tails.

'You'd just go after me,' he said. 'You'd call the cops. I know you hate me. I know you hated this.'

He entered her again through his open fly.

She stiffened as the wire tightened around her neck, felt his left hand shudder with the effort of pulling it taut, felt the blood slide down her neck and pool in the hollow of her shoulderblades.

The night went bright with flashes of yellow fire and then went dark. Her breathing stopped. Her head fell back against the moss, her body against the damp cool leaves.

Somewhere far beyond her, a man stood up and turned toward the road.

Twenty-four

They were driving again and the nausea had returned, compounded of the smell of gas and auto exhaust and blind, dark, vertiginous motion. And fear. She was getting used to feeling sick. Nausea like a *condition*, like being pregnant, like a morning sickness.

Like a hangover.

Nausea. Weakness.

Lee's arms around her weren't enough – insufficient to take her beyond herself, out of herself, or to bring her closer to him. And she wondered if they had ever been truly close, this man she had slept with and killed with and had every intention of marrying – if they lived to marry.

It seemed they had. And then it didn't.

But they must have. *Otherwise it was all . . . everything was . . .*

. . . meaningless.

And there was the fear again.

Not of Wayne this time but of sheer futility. That all this had led nowhere. Or could have led nowhere else. Her life from childhood to this moment seemed to hang over her like some sort of curse. She realized that emptiness, that lack, could be terrifying. As much as physical threat.

She wondered if this was what it felt like to be homeless, on the streets and cut adrift in the world, friendless, hopeless, alone. If this was what hostages felt like. A political prisoner held far away from home and loved ones. She felt homeless now, locked in a prison she had been making for herself her whole life long. Starting long ago, when she and her sister were just little girls.

And Lee's arms didn't help.

How could she have ever expected them to? A man's arms. Only that. She was a fool.

She remembered when they'd met at Howard's club. Memory like a vision. Had something really passed between them? Between both of them? Or had she simply sent a message and he received it? *Help. I'm vulnerable. I hate this. Take me out of here and I'm the most available woman you'll ever want to meet.*

He was not a member of the club, of course. He was there courtesy of

Howard – his new boss. Presumably the idea was for him to lose to Howard at eighteen holes of golf. Instead Lee whipped him soundly. Maybe he was already sick of Howard. It was possible. It didn't take a lot of people very long. Three weeks later they had met again in the parking lot of the Food Emporium and he asked if she'd had lunch yet. He was dressed in a sweatshirt and jeans . . . it was a Thursday, his day off. He looked nothing like Howard nor anybody who would even work for Howard, and by two in the afternoon they were in bed in his condo and by four she had told him everything.

She could feel his breath stirring her hair. His thighs pressed to her buttocks, his legs pressed to her legs.

Why wasn't it helping?

She felt abandoned.

Oh for Chrissake stop feeling so sorry for yourself, she thought.

You thought you knew the risks. You didn't. So what? It means nothing. The problem is Wayne now. Not Lee, not Howard.

Think. Concentrate.

You can live through this.

It was as though she had said it aloud.

'We have to do something,' Lee said. 'When he opens the trunk. He's going to have to help you out. You're all cramped up. I mean, even if you're not cramped up, you are – you know what I mean?'

His voice sounded raspy, his breathing shallow. He did not sound good.

'But what . . .?

'The jack's here. Maybe I can . . . use it. You'll have to distract him. Stumble. Something. I don't know. Get him off balance. Give me enough time to . . . get the son of a bitch.'

She nodded. 'Are you all right?'

'I'm okay,' he said.

For a while no one spoke.

'You think he killed her?' she said. 'The girl?'

'Yes.'

'I didn't hear anything.'

'I think he . . . took her away. Just try to give me a second where he's not looking, all right?'

'All right. Lee?'

'Yeah.'

'Why didn't we just leave?'

'Leave?'

'Why didn't we just move away from Howard? Out of Barstow. Why did we kill him?'

'I think . . .'

The car took a jolt. The jack dug into her side.

'I think we were sort of crazy,' he said. 'I think he'd made us crazy. For me, anyway . . . leaving, going away wouldn't have been enough. After what he did to you . . .I wanted him dead. I think . . . I think I maybe talked you into it. I'm sorry.'

'You didn't talk me into it, Lee.'

His arms tightened around her.

He's trying, she thought. Even trying to take the blame for her. Trying to be strong.

He didn't feel or sound strong and neither did she. Something in here was getting to them. The air-holes weren't working. They weren't enough.

She wondered about the jack. If he could handle it.

This was the part, she thought, when they were supposed to say something. They were supposed to affirm something now between them. They were supposed to say I love you and that somehow it had all been worth it.

He relaxed his embrace. They rode in silence.

WEDNESDAY MORNING

Twenty-five

The girl, Susan Olsen, had wanted to know what the mother was like.

Rule hadn't the goddamn words.

The girl was out in one of the cars now with Lieutenant Neal, who had brought over the warrant. He was going through her story again. He wouldn't get much. The girl didn't know much. Lock had kept her in the dark about a lot of things.

Like this closet.

Rule knew she had no idea.

Lock had a hobby.

He made collages. The walls of the big walk-in closet were lined with them.

Most were about two feet by three feet, photos glued to oaktag. He had cannibalized the books piled on the floor. There were a lot of them.

Torture Through History. Bloodletters and Badmen in three volumes. *Tortures And Torments of the Christian Martyrs.*

One of his favorites seemed to be a British import called *Crimes of Horror*. He'd cut out pictures of his heroes.

Manson, Bundy, Dr Crippen, Capone, Ed Gein, Albert Fish, the Vampire of Dusseldorf, Lucky Luciano.

He had photos of Jayne Mansfield's dead dog, of Bugsy Siegel shot in the head, of Paul Bern lying naked and dead in Jean Harlow's bedroom, and two different angles on Elizabeth Short – the Black Dahlia – lying neatly bisected at the waist, drained of blood and her torso mutilated lying nude in the grass, all cut from Kenneth Anger's *Hollywood Babylon* numbers one and two.

He had a book called *Violence in Our Time* which divided itself into black-and-white police- and news-photo chapters on child abuse, murder, rape, suicide, genocide, execution, assassination, terrorism, race riots, war and revolution.

There were hardly any pages in this little number left at all. They were all up there on the wall.

Dead babies – tied, beaten, burned, strangled. Shotgun blasts to the face. Self-immolations. Stabbings. Torture-crimes. Castrations. Piles of the dead at Belsen, Nordhausen, Weimar. Chinese beheadings. KKK lynchings. The hanged, stomped bodies of Mussolini and his mistress. The bodies of Cuidad Trujillo, of Nhu and Diem. A fire-blackened corpse seeming to rise from the blasted earth at Hiroshima.

Then there were the polaroids. Color shots interspersed with the black-and-white photos from the books. Some of them taken from his bedroom window, apparently, down onto the street—Rule could see the lace curtains in the foreground. Others blurred as though snapped in a hurry, furtive, surreptitious. Fugitive and without the subject's knowledge.

Kids. Old ladies. Men and women.

An equal-opportunity shooter.

He recognized only two of them.

One was the man next door, Roberts, walking his dog down on the street below.

The other was Susan Olsen.

She'd posed for this one. She was standing in a car-dealer's lot next to a highly polished Volvo, the color red. Leaning on it, wearing jeans and a yellow tank top and smiling into the camera.

She was pasted right next to the Dahlia.

You didn't have to be a genius to catch his drift. Rule was looking at a hit-list in living color.

He wondered what Susan had done to him.

He supposed he'd have to ask her.

On the bookshelf were an open box of straight-pins, a pair of wooden clothespins and a box of tissues, half-empty, and a round hand-mirror on a stand.

These, too, left a pretty clear impression.

There was nothing much else of interest either in here or in the rest of the house so far. They'd been through most of it by now. It was neat. Even tidy. So much so that you'd think a woman still lived here.

It was sexist but too bad.

He walked down the stairs to the two Mutt-and-Jeff uniformed officers standing in the living room.

'Where's Lieutenant Covitski?'

The taller one pointed toward the kitchen.

'Basement,' he said.

The kitchen was tidy too. Not a dish in the sink. The sponge looked like he'd never used it.

Covitski was just coming up the stairs. He was smiling.

'He's got a freezer down there. You know what's in it?'

'You mean what? Not who?'

Covitski laughed. 'Spinach, asparagus and broccoli. That's all. Nothing else. Must have thirty boxes each in there.'

'He likes his veggies.'

'And doesn't like variety.'

'Take a look in the bedroom closet,' he said. 'It's interesting.'

'But no gun, right?' said Covitski.

'No gun.'

'He's got it with him. We're not gonna find a thing here.'

'Looks that way. Listen, I want to talk to the girl again. I don't expect much but why not. Then, unless she surprises me I think maybe we should go home and get some sleep. Let Neal and the uniforms handle interviewing the neighbors and stake out the house. He's fresh. I'm feeling a little brain-dead here. Two hours on the sofa would feel like a miracle. What do you say?'

'I say Jesus, fine. Great.'

They'd been on for sixteen, almost seventeen hours and they'd done whatever it was they could do here. It was definitely time to call it quits a while.

'Check the closet,' he said.

Covitski grinned. 'Get to know your rabbit, huh?' he said.

'We damn well better get to know this one,' he said, and went out to the prowl car where the girl was sitting in the back seat looking anxious and bewildered, Jack Neal sitting beside her glancing down at a pad that was practically empty.

He decided that if she asked him what they found in there he'd tell her. She had the right of any victim to know. He thought a moment of Ann in California and opened the door opposite Neal and sat down beside her, the girl between them smelling of fresh tears and faint cologne, and started going through it all again, the litany of emptiness that was the woman's life with a man who had her photo pinned to his wall surrounded by death and who she'd thought she loved.

Twenty-six

It was possible to turn to her left and get to her knees.

The forest swam. Her body ached and stung.

She began by using her fingernails on the twisted wire around her wrist. It was sticky with blood. The wrist was swollen so that the wire had cut deep.

When the first wrist was free she worked at the other one until finally the wire dropped away gleaming wetly in the moonlight, coiled around the birch tree. She reached up for the second length wrapped around her neck and pulled it gently free.

The bleeding immediately began anew. She could taste it in her mouth. There was no way to know how badly he had hurt her. She could feel the blood roll down across her collarbone. She found she could painfully swallow.

She didn't try to stand. She was still too weak for that. Instead she reached for her clothes, leaned back against the tree and put on her shoes and cutoffs and slipped her arms into the shirtsleeves.

She rested. She buttoned the shirt.

She stood slowly, using the tree for balance until her legs felt strong enough to support her, and then moved off through the forest.

She was going to survive again.

Her luck, whatever it was, was holding.

And she wondered for a while, before she found her anger again, why it felt so bad, so terrible to know that. Until the feeling bled away into the heat of her living body, into a grim determination to stop him, cancel him, to make him pay. She would do what she could to make him pay.

She stumbled through the forest toward the moonlight shining bright across the empty road ahead and sorted through every moment, every word, since he'd pulled up across the road from them and began what she – not he – would finish.

That this took courage did not even occur to her.

She embraced his image like a lover, and remembered.

136

Twenty-seven

Wayne's was not anyone's notion of a mind at peace. It had never been.

His mind was always busy – devising, sorting, cataloging, planning and unplanning – despite what was going on, despite what he happened to be doing or who he happened to be with, despite flu or headache or sleepless nights. It churned all day long. Sorting and sifting even through his dreams. As though his mind ran on its own tenacious frequency regardless of the presence of all that which composed him yet which was not mind. Regardless, in other words, of his physical self.

He was rarely to be found exactly *inside* his experiences.

Still, now, driving the deserted two-lane Governor-something Highway to Lake Winnipesaukee and Wolfeboro, he felt a kind of peace. Perhaps mind and body had found a link they had not had up to now. Perhaps they were finally in synch.

Perhaps his dick had at long last caught up with his brain.

He cruised close to the waterline, a happy man.

Buzzing.

Twenty-eight

'Jesus, Rule – it's what? Two-thirty in the morning? Go back to bed!'

'I haven't been to bed. I fucked up, Marty.'

'What?'

Rule could hear his therapist sigh at the other end and then the bed creaking and the match lighting and the sharp intake of breath.

'I fucked up. With Ann.'

Three beers and he was a little drunk. Even to himself he sounded maudlin. *You're a cop,* he thought. Jesus, *stop whining.* He couldn't help it.

'I don't know why I know that but I do,' he said. 'I fucked up. I just thought I'd tell you.'

'This couldn't wait for our session?'

'It's the nature of the business, Marty. There might not be a session. You never can say. I thought you'd want something to remember me by. Introspective breakthrough. Just in case.'

'Bullshit, Rule.'

'Not necessarily. There's a very mean man out there with a gun.'

'Mean men with guns are your business, Rule. You like your business. What's so special about this one?'

'He's involved somebody else, I guess. Somebody who reminds me of Ann every which way, every damn time I turn around and look at it.'

'So this is sort of personal.'

'In a way. Yeah.'

'And it's not supposed to be personal. Personal could be dangerous.'

'It could be.'

'So you want my advice.'

'I don't know about that. That's not why I called.'

'You wanted to tell me something about Ann.'

'Right.'

'So go ahead. I've got no worries about the other thing. You'll depersonalize this when you have to. You'll live.'

He let that go.

'I just figure I fucked up, Marty. I could have gone with her. Or else I

138

could have created a situation so she'd stay. What I mean is I could have effected things. Instead I just let it drift and then I cut her loose, I left her all alone out there. I threw the whole damn thing into the fireplace. After six years I left her and Chrissie all alone because *I* had to be alone to really feel secure for some reason and if they don't hate me for it then they damn well ought to. She could be the best thing that ever happened to me, Marty.'

'She could be. But it seems to me that Ann had some say in this too, didn't she?'

'Sure she did. She said she wanted me. Only not on the same old idiotic terms. And the old terms were the only terms I could offer. At the time.'

'And now?'

'Now I'm not so sure.'

Marty sighed. 'Rule, go chase your bad guy. You're in the middle of something here, am I right? So go and finish it. Then we'll talk and we'll see if anything's changed, okay?'

'Yeah. All right.'

'And Rule?'

'Yeah.'

'You want my opinion I think you're still afraid you'll lose her. That's a little perverse, Rule. Because – we already talked about this – you've already lost her. Accept it. She has.'

He didn't know what to say. He just seemed to melt down into the bed like it was some weird sort of relief to hear Marty tell him that but it was also like the clap of doom.

'And Rule?'

'Yeah?'

'When I want something to remember you by, I'll ask for it. You know?'

'Yeah.'

'Okay. Goodnight, Lieutenant.'

'Goodnight, Marty.'

He went out to the garage. He lit a cigarette in the dark and stared at the dolls' house for a while. He could probably finish it off in two or three weekends if he gave it a try, pack it up and send it off to them.

He wondered if he'd do that.

He finished the smoke and lit another. Thinking that the dolls' house looked really good there.

Ten minutes later his phone rang.

He didn't suppose it was Marty phoning him back.

Twenty-nine

At three-fifteen Covitski was dreaming about a bust.

Not his wife Mae's lying there dreaming beside him, which was substantial. No. A burglary bust.

Somebody had broken into a home very much like the Gardner home and had stolen the following: one hundred dollars in rolled-up quarters, untraceable, a thousand dollars' worth of ladies' shoes and steaks from the downstairs freezer, also untraceable, five thousand dollars' worth of camera gear and computer equipment, very rough to trace if the guy was any good at his work – and a parrot.

Hell, they were never going to find *any* of this shit!

And then there he is walking by the *Tats Are Us* Tattoo Emporium – which didn't exist – it seems like only a second later, the fastest investigation in the history of the world, and he sees this parrot in the window.

He opens the door and the parrot is whistling. The theme is instantly familiar. The owner of the parrot, the shoes, the steaks, the electronics gear and the rolls of quarters has told him the parrot sings *exactly this song*! And *only* this song. The theme from *The Andy Griffith Show*. Da-da-*DAT-DAA*-da-da-dat-*DAA*-da-da-dat . . .

He makes his arrest on the spot.

It's a moment to remember. A moment of absolute purity, of happiness and yes, it's time to party!

When his phone rings.

Not in his dream but in real life, such as it is.

Mae rolls over. 'God damn it,' she mutters. She adjusts her curlers on the side she's sleeping on now and before Covitski can get the phone off the stand and up to his ear she's out again.

God bless her.

'Yeah.'

It's Rule.

'Covitski, we're on again.'

'Ah Jesus . . .'

'We got a witness to murder, Covitski. And Lock's gone interstate.'

'He's interstate?'

140

'Right.'

'How do we know?'

'Girl and her boyfriend met up with him just outside of Plymouth some time before midnight, eleven-thirty maybe. He pulled a gun on them but used a hammer on the boyfriend. Raped her and left her there for dead. Plymouth DA's office says she's talking a blue streak, enough particulars to convict him half a dozen times, mad as hell and tough as they come.

'The thing I don't like, she says he was alone. No passengers.'

'No Gardner and no Edwards.'

'Right. But then, get this. They had a drive-by in Hanover just a while earlier. Some kid. Right in the goddamn center of town. Weapon, a .357 magnum . . .'

'So *there's* the magnum! He's screwing around with weapons, with MOs.'

'That's right.'

'Any ID on the car?'

'Nobody saw it. But you can bet it's our guy. Listen, I'm leaving now. How soon can you meet me?'

'I can be out of here in ten, fifteen minutes.'

'Try for ten, okay?'

'You got it.'

He slipped his pants over the day-old shorts. Who gave a shit.

Two more dead, he thought. Some poor girl raped. And the two passengers, male and female, disappeared.

It was fucking grim. It really was.

Still – he could almost hear the parrot.

Thirty

Wayne turned on the overhead light.
　　He took out his pad.
　　He began to read the names.

Thirty-one

Lepke radioed it in just past the New Hampshire state border near Bradford and read them the plates.

He had his instructions. *Follow, do not apprehend. Repeat. Do not apprehend.*

That was fine with him.

They were sending in the troops. Fine.

He was a highway cop in a cruiser. Nobody told him that hero was part of the job description.

He wondered if the guy in the Volvo was headed back to Barstow. You never knew with loonies. And judging from the dispatches this one was a certified Toon. Drive-bys, rape. The whole nine yards.

He was tailing one of the bad guys. One of the *real* bad guys. It felt pretty good.

There was nobody much on the road so he dropped back aways. So far he felt sure the guy hadn't made him but he was riding a cherry and the guy wasn't blind. There was somebody coming up behind him, moving slowly up on his left, he could see the headlights in the rear-view mirror. Maybe he could get this citizen here between them. He'd be much less conspicuous. He dropped back.

The citizen was driving a brand-new Mazda, blue. Lepke glanced over. A male suit in his late forties. The guy crept past Lepke the way they always do passing a cop, signaled nicely and got into lane ahead of him.

Very good.

And they cruised along that way for a while.

Then the Mazda got antsy. You couldn't blame him – the Volvo wasn't exactly going hell bent for leather, the guy was doing maybe five to seven under the limit. The Mazda signaled and pulled out into the fast lane.

Lepke watched him crawl up parallel to the Volvo, real slow, still aware of the cruiser behind him.

Watch, he thought, another mile or so, another hill between them, and the Mazda would be up to seventy. Like Lepke wouldn't know this. Like all cops are dummies.

He could scoot over the hill and take the Mazda in three minutes flat.

He was thinking this and picturing it and thinking that another time and he'd have done exactly that when something that sounded like a fucking cannon went off ahead of him, *Jesus*! and he saw the glint of metal out the Volvo's driver's-side window and saw the splash of glass and something else, something dark and wet, bursting out of the Mazda.

And then three things happened simultaneously.

The Mazda started to drift, decelerating rapidly but still doing maybe forty, forty-five, toward the metal guardrail that separated the northbound from the southbound lanes. The guy was leaning on his horn. Something was.

And the Volvo was picking up speed. Fifty-five. Sixty. Sixty-five on the radar. And Lepke had to wonder if the guy hadn't made him as a cop from square one.

He was reaching for his mike and hitting the emergency channel and tromping on the gas pedal himself, deciding he had no choice now but to go after the crazy bastard, when the Mazda hit the rail.

And the timing was all fucked up.

Because the Mazda ground screeching, sparks flying, up against the rail for five or six feet and then turned and drifted back aimless as a poleaxed steer into his lane at about thirty miles per hour, did this just as Lepke was about to pass him – and he couldn't judge whether to hit the brakes or not it was so fast and close so he just kept going, accelerating, going after the son of a bitch, praying that this speed was exactly the right speed, and he heard his call numbers on the radio *come in come in* as the Mazda rammed his door and caved it in on him.

He felt his legs go first and then his ribs and then his forearm snap against the steering wheel, all in rapidfire succession, the steering wheel snapping too, and then he was spinning in some screeching-metal waltz with the Mazda a full three hundred and sixty degrees and there were flames licking at him bursting over him pinned there, clothes going, seared into his body, *becoming* his body, hair going, eyes already beginning to fucking fry inside him as he screamed and writhed and screamed and glanced through the splintered windshield and saw the last thing he would ever see.

The empty highway. The hill. The Volvo gone.

Thirty-two

There was as much energy in the room as Rule had ever seen there and it was four in the morning.

Hamsun was in his cubicle with the door wide open, called in with no more sleep that Rule had gotten which was none, on the phone to the State Highway Patrol. There were cops on phones taking reports, and other cops filing them, typewriters going like a secretarial pool. Somehow the press had got wind of it and papers were calling from as far away as New York City. The phones were ringing like they were holding a telethon in there.

Wayne-Aid.

When Covitski walked in he'd just gotten off the line to Bradford.

'You ready?' he said. 'He killed a cop.'

'He what?'

'He killed a cop.' Rule gave him the thumbnail. 'Look,' he said.

He got up and walked to the wall-map.

'This guy is pretty strange. First we make him here on 89 heading down toward Montpelier. Then he's across the state line into Hanover, he shoots the kid there with the magnum. Next he's all the way over in Plymouth. Rapes one student, kills another. And finally here. Across the line again out of Bradford.'

'He's making a circle.'

'Looks like it. He sure as hell isn't headed for Mexico.'

'What've we got going?'

'We've got cars at his house, the Gardner place, Susan Olsen's, and his mother's rest home – though *that's* one hell of a long shot. We've got an interstate APB so that the entire east coast from DC up to Canada is keeping an eye out for him.

'A red Volvo, for Chrissake. The crazy son of a bitch doesn't even have the sense to switch cars.

'And the feds are in this too. Once he crossed the border with Gardner and Edwards he bought himself a federal kidnap rap along with everything else. It's a matter of time. We'll get him.'

'What now?'

'We do what everybody else is doing. We answer the phone. We wait.

145

The feds will be over in about,' he checked his watch, 'twenty minutes. Pick our brains. Wonderful, right? You want some coffee?'

'I'm thinking about Edwards and the Gardner woman. It doesn't look good, does it?'

'No. Not with five dead that we know of it doesn't.'

The phone rang. Covitski sat down and picked it up.

'Black,' he said.

'Huh?'

'The coffee. Make it black.'

Thirty-three

He saw them the moment he turned onto his street. The car was unmarked but he knew who they were.

He could practically smell them.

He cut his lights and crawled to a stop. Parked the Volvo half a block down.

He reached into the back seat, found what he needed and then got out and quietly closed the door.

He heard someone pounding inside on the lid of the trunk. That meant they were still alive. He was glad they were alive. He wanted them alive.

His witnesses.

The streetlight had gone out a week ago and no one had been around to fix it yet. That was a problem living in this part of town. But now, of course, it was all to his advantage. He thought that even the town itself was playing right into his hands.

It was only right. The town belonged to him.

He stayed close to the hedges. There was a little boy and a little girl living here in this house. Twins. They were probably seven years old. Across the street a pair of old ladies, spinsters. He kept moving.

He stopped in front of the Crocker house. The woman was named Rebecca and the man was called Lance. What in hell kind of a name was *Lance*? They kept a nice place, you had to give them that. The lawn was neatly trimmed. He would see the man out there mowing every Saturday.

They were in his book, though, because of the name. The name offended him.

The car was directly in front of him, parked by Ed Schorr's. Ed was all right. He worked in the post office. Whenever he went in there for stamps or something Ed was very efficient and had a pleasant manner. It was his wife who was a bitch. She wore too-tight dresses and too much makeup and when you smiled at her she didn't smile back. Like she was somebody. And not the wife of some fucking postal clerk.

The two policemen were sitting with the windows open, the idiots. Of course it was hot. But they were making it easy. He knew exactly how it was going to play.

147

He stepped over.

Treat and Burkeman were still fresh.

They were used to the night shift and they'd only been sitting there an hour and a half. In fact Treat, behind the wheel, still had almost half a cup of Seven-Eleven coffee in his hand.

Burkeman had finished his, along with a jellyroll and a two-pack of Twinkies. Burkeman liked junk food, which partly accounted for the fact that at thirty-three he still had problems with his complexion. Zits grew on him during the night like toadstools. He kept his face scrupulously clean but it didn't help. Zits liked him. What could you do?

They were talking about Willie Bly, a cop who had unloaded on a bunch of teenagers three nights earlier after sitting at Logan's all day drinking whiskey. Yelling at the kids, calling them every name in the book because they were out there smoking cigarettes and leaning on his ten-year-old Chevy when he came out of the bar. Bly loved that Chevy and he hated teenagers. The fact that he had three of his own probably had something to do with it.

The teenagers complained to their parents and their parents complained to Bly's supervisor and now Bly was suspended for a week. The fact that one of the kids was a councilman's daughter probably had something to do with that too.

Burkeman thought it was unfair. But Treat held that Bly was going to have to learn to keep his trap shut someday anyhow – did Burkeman remember when Bly called Hamsun, a fucking captain for Chrissake, *that lard-ass no-Dick Tracy?*

In front of half the squad-room?

Burkeman did, and they were laughing over that and Treat was sipping at his tepid coffee when the guy came out of nowhere and leaned in through Burkeman's window, smiling, and stabbed him in the throat with an eight-inch high-carbon stainless steel kitchen knife, pushed it all the way through so that Treat was looking at three inches of bloody steel sticking out of his partner's neck as he dropped his coffee and reached for his gun and the guy brought up his other hand and popped him one in the forehead.

Burkeman was still alive then, barely, knife and all. Enough so that he saw the two inches of green rubber garden hose the guy had used as a home-made silencer fall off into his lap, thinking, *Jesus I'm fucked, I'm truly fucked,* and then *What the hell is that?* as he looked down stunned at the length of hose and Treat bounced off the driver's-side door and slumped over onto Burkeman's shoulder, a neat little hole in the center of his forehead oozing blood. He had just time to be aware of all this, hands moving sluggish, slow-motion to his neck, when the guy reached in and took the handle of the knife and pulled it forward. He felt his windpipe go and the guy tugged again and he saw the spray.

And that was that, thought Wayne, for their silly outpost.

Thirty-four

Carole heard the key slip into the lock and felt Lee gently squeeze her hand.

In the instant before the trunk lid opened she was a little girl again, huddling close to her older sister Alex in the dark.

The door to their bedroom was about to open. Their father was about to enter.

Their father was a teacher of high school math – later, when Carole was a teenager, he would become principal – a tall thin man with glasses and dark wavy hair. A little like Dennis' dad in *Dennis the Menace*. Until he was principal and his hair went gray and white.

Her father would enter in his pyjamas and whisper to one of them, Alex or Carole, and one of them would get out of bed and follow him through the darkened hallway past the bedroom where her mother lay sleeping into the guestroom which was not really a guestroom but where her father slept most nights, and he would pull back the covers for her and she would climb into bed. The bed smelled of her father who would stand watching her in the doorway until she either fell asleep again or pretended to, and then he would climb in beside her. Moments later he would begin touching her, hesitantly at first, and then probing deeply with his fingers, and Carole or Alex would try very hard not to cry.

It's all right, he would say. *Daddy loves you. Daddy will always love you. You're a good girl. You're a good girl now.*

In the moment before the trunk opened out to the reality of the street her sister gripped her hand one last time.

Then there was Wayne smiling in at them.

His hands were stained and glistening. He held the small .38 in his right hand. The suitcase sat beside him next to the curb.

'Help,' she said. 'I need your hand.'

It was true. She wasn't lying. She could not have gotten out of there without him. Her head swam. More so now with the sudden rush of air. Her bones felt thin and brittle inside her.

She reached for his hand.

'Help me.'

She could see him hesitate for a moment.

Then he took it.

She managed to straighten out her right leg slightly and slip it over the rim of the compartment, using his grip for balance so she wouldn't fall back onto Lee.

He pulled her forward and she felt her foot touch the street and then her body was following, unfolding, drifting out of the compartment toward him, the leg scraping painfully down over the bumper and then almost buckling at the ankle as it received the full weight of her.

He pulled harder and her lungs filled with the warm fresh air as her left foot snagged on the rim, the toe of her shoe not quite making it over and her free hand darting out to him, to the shoulder of his gun hand, grasping at his shoulder, falling toward him, drunk on fresh sudden air, catching hold of his shirt and clutching it and this was no trick, she was actually falling, this was not what they had planned. Irony upon irony, it was absolutely real.

She heard him swear. And instead of supporting her felt him shift to the side and pull suddenly away, releasing his grip on her hand as her own clenched fingers lost the fabric of his shirt and slid uselessly down over his chest.

She felt him wrap the arm of his gun hand around her waist and pivot and hurl her away from him toward the street and the raised yellow curb, heard him shout and knew that Lee had done something after all, something with the jack from the trunk.

Then the curb loomed. And struck her like a stone.

Lee half shoved it, half flung it at him.

The jack caught him square in the hip, crack of bone and loud metallic clatter as it fell to the street. He saw Carole hurtling toward the curb as Wayne stumbled with the impact and his own momentum, hurt, almost but not quite losing it, almost falling, and he was out of the car on legs that felt like an old man's legs, going for the gun.

The gun came up to meet him.

He heard his cheekbone shatter.

He fell and barely caught himself on the rim of the trunk. Thinking, *Ah no ah Jesus Carole we fucked up*. Not even hurting yet. Not even worrying about her. Just *we fucked up*.

He turned. Staring into the short round barrel of the automatic.

'You assholes,' said Wayne. 'Look what you did.'

He looked.

She was lying in the gutter.

There were leaves and twigs in there and some kind of candy or cigarette wrapper and her legs didn't look right. They were splayed and there was no dignity to them and no beauty with her skirt up around her waist, and the angle looked all wrong to him.

Oh, God, he thought.

Her arms were wrong too. One up over her head, her hand up over the curb like she was pawing her way toward the grass beyond it and the other lying palm-up, fingers crooked at her side. Her long hair whipped out in front of her as though she were someone captured in a photo – a woman surprised by a heavy wind that had come at her and caught her from behind.

'Real nice work,' Wayne said.

'Fuck you.' *Fawwk eeuuu.*

His jaw worked against the muscles of his cheek and the cheekbone screamed raw broken pain.

Wayne did not seem to mind being cursed at this time.

'Get up,' he sighed. 'Go see if she's alive or dead or what.'

He got up and walked over. Knelt unsteadily beside her.

In the moonlight the top of her head looked black. He could see the thick steady ooze of blood. He felt for a pulse in her neck.

Thank God.

'Doctor,' he said. 'She needs a doctor.'

'Not a hearse?' Wayne smiled. 'Lucky you. Pick her up.'

'Shouldn't move her.'

'Pick her up you fucking little traitor or I will kill your traitorous ass right here and she can get up and get her own fucking doctor. Do it!'

He didn't want to touch her – for all they knew her neck could be broken – he didn't want to touch her much less pick her up but there was still no arguing with the gun and however bad this was they both were still alive. He lifted her head, bent down and angled it so that it lay against his chest, got one arm up under her legs and the other across her back and lifted with his legs. They barely took the burden.

Lee stood and turned and faced him. He could feel the wetness spreading across his shirt.

'Where . . .?' he said.

'Home,' said Wayne.

He picked up his suitcase and motioned with the gun.

'We're going home, Lee. At least I am. You? I don't know *where* you're going. I honestly don't. I really wish I knew.'

Thirty-five

'He tried to choke me once,' said Susan.

'When was this?'

Okay. We're finally getting down to it, he thought. Down to why she'd left him.

On everything else Rule had found the girl thoroughly cooperative. On this subject only she was still evasive. Even after knowing why they were looking for Wayne. But now she was sitting at his desk drinking coffee and she had this determined look on her face and he knew she was working on it and working through whatever was making her reluctant.

He didn't press her. He waited.

'Just last Saturday,' she said. 'We were . . . having sex.'

There you go, he thought.

'And he tried to choke you?'

'We were making love and he was . . . and everything was perfectly normal. Then all of a sudden he just started choking me.'

'And this was where? Your place or Wayne's?'

She shook her head.

'Neither. We were on the mountain. At the Notch.'

'The Notch?'

'We were hiking. We'd brought a picnic. We were going up to the pond. Then I got tired and we stopped and there was nobody around anywhere . . . so we . . . so I . . . we started making love.'

He couldn't believe it. He wanted to say, *You* thought *you were alone up there* but he didn't.

He had a very good idea what was coming next.

'Susan, when he did this to you . . . *after* he did this to you, what did you do?'

'I got mad. I got absolutely furious. I left him.'

'You left him?' She nodded. 'You went back down the mountain?'

'That's right.'

'And what did he do then?'

'I don't know. I haven't talked to him at all since then. Stayed up there, I guess. I mean, he didn't try to follow me or anything. Why?'

Wayne had hung around. He'd seen them. He was not an accomplice. He'd seen them murder Howard and then he'd gotten to them somehow. It was all a nasty piece of luck but it was all in place now.

'Susan, would you mind if I call Lieutenant Covitski in on this? I know it's tough for you but . . .'

'I don't mind. The hard time was *this* time, you know what I mean?'

He knew. And he could have kissed her. He went and got Covitski.

Thirty-six

'Set her there,' he said. He pointed to the couch. 'No, hold on a minute. Come here. Walk.' He pushed the magnum into the small of Lee's back and walked him through the living room down a short hall into the kitchen. He opened a drawer and took out a handful of white linen towels.

'Okay, back,' he said.

In the living room he folded two of the towels in half and spread them out on a pillow on the couch. Lee put her down. The right side of his shirt was soaked through with blood from his shoulder to his belt.

'Here,' he said. He handed him a towel. 'Wrap her head.'

Her eyelids fluttered.

He folded the linen as Wayne had done, laid it across the top of her head over the wound and tied it beneath her chin. The blood started seeping through.

'Not enough,' he said. 'We need a doctor.'

'Here.'

He handed him another towel. It was something. Lee tied it over the first one. He pressed it down gently with his hand, trying to stop the bleeding, all the time thinking, *concussion* – how hard is too hard? Goddammit I have no idea what I'm doing here.

'See? Better.'

'It's *not* better. Jesus! She could *die*, Wayne!'

He seemed to consider that.

'Did I tell you I was once a paramedic, Lee?'

'Bullshit.'

'No, it's true. I did it for about a year or so. Then I got bored.'

'*Bored*, Wayne?'

He seemed to realize that the choice of words was the wrong one, a very long stretch of logic.

Lee felt his face flush. He'd like to have torn this guy limb from limb.

He thought he could do anything, this bastard. Get away with anything!

'Don't argue with me, Lee. If I say I was a paramedic then I was. *I'll*

155

take care of her. We don't need any goddamn doctor. Now take her clothes off. We'll have a look.'

'What?'

'We'll check her out.'

'Fuck you.'

'Did you take her pulse? *No*. Did you listen to her heartbeat? No. See? You don't know anything! Better yet, move over away from there. *I'll* do it.'

'The hell you will.'

'The hell I won't, Lee.' He held up the magnum.

Lee got to his feet. Finally sick of him. *Sick to goddamn death of him.*

'You use that thing and you'll wake the neighbors for miles around. You'll have the police here in minutes.'

Wayne reached around into his back pocket.

'I'll use this, then.'

He put the magnum down on the table beside him and pointed the .38, reached into his pants and took out what looked like a piece of green rubber tubing, black and exploded at the end. He fitted it onto the gunbarrel.

'And this will make it quieter.'

'I thought you wanted us alive, Wayne.'

'I did. Then you two had to go fuck it up. You went after me. I thought we could all be buddies but all you wanted to do was hurt me from the start and do me harm.'

'*We* wanted to hurt *you*.'

'That's right.'

Keep him talking, he thought.

The magnum was down now. Not far.

Get closer.

He took a step.

'I think it's been the other way around, Wayne.'

'I couldn't give a shit what you think, Lee.'

'I thought we were supposed to be witnesses. Witnesses to what, Wayne?'

'*To me*, you asshole! *TO ME!* Don't you understand *anything*?'

'Why? Are you supposed to be some kind of natural phenomenon or something? Like the weather?'

'YES! Yes *exactly*! Like the weather, Lee! Like a goddamn *storm*! *I'm* the storm! The one that blows it all away, that tears down all the houses, that crushes all you little assholes inside! That takes away everything you've got including your miserable fucking stupid empty lives! You got it now? *You got that?*'

What you did with a storm was you waited for it to blow out.

I can outthink this son of a bitch, he thought. I can maneuver him. And I can live.

Control.

'You got it?'

'Yes. I think so, Wayne,' he said.

Use his name.

He took a step and held out his hand. He kept it low and non-threatening. Held it out palm-up.

'Listen, Wayne, I don't want to cross you. I don't want to harm you. You've got us both wrong. Figure it out. What would you do if you were us? Wouldn't you try to get free? You promised to let us go. But you didn't. You put us in the goddamn trunk of a *car*, Wayne. Wouldn't you try to get free after that if you were me?'

'I might.'

'So?'

Wayne just stared at him. He could read nothing from the man, no feeling whatsoever one way or the other.

He sighed. 'Listen, could I ... would you mind if I had a smoke, Wayne? I'm out. Have you got one? Jesus, I don't know what to think about all this. I just know I could use a smoke.'

'Don't fuck with me, Lee.'

'I wouldn't fuck with you, Wayne. I'm asking for a cigarette. That's all.'

'What about her?'

He nodded toward Carole.

'Do what you want, Wayne, Go ahead. Take her clothes off. You say you're a paramedic and if you say so then maybe you are. I honestly don't care anymore. I've had it. I'm exhausted.'

A step. To the side this time. Not pushing him. Don't push him. To the side but a little closer.

The magnum gleaming in the light from the table-lamp in front of him.

The empty ceramic ashtray sitting right beside it.

Cigarettes and ashtrays.

'So how about the smoke?'

Wayne's eyes narrowed. His lips turned up at the corners in what he guessed was supposed to be a smile.

'Fuck the smoke, Lee. You don't want the smoke. You want the gun. You want the gun? Then go for it.'

'I don't want the gun.'

'Yes you do. You're going to be a hero now. Aren't you?'

'No.'

'Of course you are.'

'It's not what I had in mind, Wayne.'

'What did you have in mind?'

'A cigarette.'

'A cigarette.'

'That's right.'

'You're a liar, Lee. Suppose we go back to plan one. You strip the bitch and I have a look at her.'

It's not supposed to go this way, he thought. How could Wayne see through him like this? It wasn't the first time he'd done it either. It was as though the guy had some secret track into his mind. Reading him, constantly reading him. It was scary as hell.

'I just don't want to do that, Wayne.'

'Why not?'

'Could I just have the cigarette?'

'You're saying no to me, Lee?'

'Look. I'm not . . . yes. I guess I am. On this one I am. I guess I'm saying no to you, Wayne.'

'Why?'

'*Why?* For Christ's sake!'

He was losing it. He was not supposed to lose control but this guy could push buttons where he didn't even know he had buttons. It was somehow necessary to him that Carole's clothes stay exactly as they were, where they were. Why was that? What could it matter? Wayne was going to do what he was going to do unless he could reach the gun and for that he needed control.

'I think what you're trying to do here, Lee, is you're trying to make things normal again and be my buddy again or something, you're trying to lull me. Just a smoke between friends, that sort of thing.

'But it's too late, Lee. We passed that.

'The bitch is going to die. You realize that?'

Concentrate, he thought. There's got to be a way. Don't let him get to you. Forget about Carole. You have to. It's just the two of us now. It has to be.

'I'm going to sit here and *watch* her die.'

His face went dreamy.

'It should be interesting, you know? She'll be naked. I'll watch. Her breathing will get more and more shallow. Her breasts will rise and fall. Rise and fall.

'Then they just . . . won't anymore.

'They'll get cold. Turn white. Blue and white. The blood will drain away . . .

'So. Want to hang around and join me?

158

'Want to watch?

'Still want to be *buddies*, Lee?'

It was impossible.

He felt the imperative turning like a waterwheel inside him. Electric energy, roaring water.

There was only one way to relieve the pressure and that was to shoot him and see him die.

He dove for the table.

He heard the gun go off, something spitting across the few feet of floor space and into his chest, knocking him away. He reached for the leg of the table, twisted and pulled and the table fell, the lamp smashing, bulb popping, spraying Wayne's feet with shattered glass as the magnum bounced once on the throw rug, its grip striking the rug and spinning it toward him.

He reached and found it with icy fingers as Wayne's gun went off a second time and he felt the bullet strike his chest not an inch from the first one directly above it like he was a cardboard target in a shooting gallery. His fingers went numb, the heavy handle slipped away, the numbness spreading through his chest and his arm from the shoulder on down and he turned, twisted, trying to grab at it with his left hand but it was out of reach.

He fell back and saw Wayne fire one last time, felt the uncanny accuracy of it slapping into him in a tight triangular pattern and looked down at himself, his blood mixed with her blood spreading out all across his chest.

He thought, Look what I've done.

He thought, You'll never see any doctor now oh Jesus, surprised that as he lay dying this thought was in fact for her and not for him at all and saddened, so late, finally to learn that he was capable of that.

Look, he thought. Look what I've done to you.

Look.

Thirty-seven

He wrapped another towel around her head. He didn't want to stain the couch.

He took the top button of her dress between thumb and index finger and slid it slowly through the buttonhole. And the next. And the next. He took his time.

He parted the dress away. The thin pale lavender bra hooked in front, He snapped it free.

'You lied,' he said.

She had said there were no scars yet there were scars, in particular a thin white line that ran from the center of her chest across her right breast and through the nipple, disappearing down the slope of the breast on the other side.

He slipped off her shoes and put them next to Lee lying slumped against the couch at his feet.

The panties matched the bra. They were thin and lacy. He slid them down off her hips, folded them once and placed them beside the shoes.

Dawn was breaking.

Her skin seemed to glow in its pale light. There was virtually no tan line. It was possible to think, looking at her flesh, that she was already dead. He could see her shallow breathing and knew this wasn't true. But the notion delighted him. He thought that even with the towels and the clotted blood on her face that she was very pretty.

So pretty the dead. So vulnerable.

His unbuckled his belt. Unzipped his pants and slid them off.

To fuck the dead and dying.

He lowered himself down.

Her skin still felt so warm. It spoiled the illusion. It was good skin, soft. Smooth as Susan's had been though Carole was probably ten years older. But he had expected a coolness from all that loss of blood. Some slight chill at least. More of an approximation.

He wasn't hard.

Not nearly hard enough.

It surprised him.

160

That bitch back off the road in Plymouth, he thought. That bitch's fault.

She'd drained him.

He bit at the scar to make himself hard.

Her body never stirred.

In that respect at least it was almost as though she *were* dead.

And thinking that he finally began to rise. He tried to push himself inside her but she was much too dry so he licked the palm of his hand until it was slick with spit and rubbed himself and tried again.

It wasn't working.

God dammit!

It was Carole who was doing this. Carole doing this to him. Not the Plymouth whore.

Fucking Carole.

Fucking Carole on his case again.

Let us go. No no. You can't do that. I won't *do that.*

Bitch!

He bit down at the scar until he could taste her blood but it didn't do his cock any good at all, the bitch was just lying there doing nothing for him, nothing, there was no excitement, no thrill, no pleasure in her anywhere. It was no goddamn good.

He wasn't stupid. He knew she was trying to defeat him again the same way she'd tried to defeat him at the bar, refusing to go over to the couple at the table next to them but he'd shown her then, he'd blown away six or seven people since then yes it was seven counting Lee and he could damn well show her again.

Show everybody.

'Fuck *you*,' he said. 'Fuck all of you!'

He shoved himself off and stood over her and slapped her hard across the face. Her blood splattered the sofa, a red mist across the faded chintz pattern.

She made no sound.

It was frustrating that she could be so unaware of him after all this time. He realized that scaring the hell out of her and Lee had been tremendous fun. Tremendous fun.

He almost missed them.

Christ! Look at the goddamn *mess* she was making!

He pushed back the coffee table, lifted her off the couch and dumped her on the floor. It would be easier to clean up the floor than the couch later after he was through.

Fuck her, he thought.

Let her lie there and just drop quietly dead.

161

He didn't need to see. It would have been nice to see her die but he had other priorities.

She was nothing.

Lee was nothing.

There were others.

He didn't even need to consult the book. He had it all in his head. He always had. The book was just to remind him.

RETAL.

He pulled up his pants and belted them. He took the .38 off the table and checked the load and the load was down so he opened the suitcase and took out a fresh clip, inserted it and stuffed six more clips into his pockets. It was too bad he didn't have more shells for the magnum but he had used them sparingly and by his count he had six rounds left in that gun too.

He looked at himself in the living room mirror.

Here I am friends and neighbors.

Mister Disaster. The guy who lives to blow your ass away. The guy who loves you, blood and bone.

It's payback time.

One holy hell of a *good* time. Was had by all.

Here I come.

He laughed and then stopped laughing. He opened the door and stepped out into the dawn, stood for a moment in the warm morning breeze scented with dew already baking off the grass, gazed around him at his home, at his white birch castle walls and then walked toward the street.

Thirty-eight

'Burkeman and Treat,' said Rule. 'They haven't made their half-hour call-in and we can't kick them up on the radio.'

He stood in front of Covitski with his hands on the desk and Covitski couldn't tell if it was just the lack of sleep that was making Rule's eyes that red or something else but the eyes were wild whatever it was.

'Something's going down. We've got an all-cars out to the Lock place. Let's go.'

Covitski was already on his feet.

Outside they saw Susan Olsen waiting for her cab. They'd offered a ride earlier but she'd turned them down. Now it was just as well. Every car they had was the car that might just get there first.

She'd noticed them too. Covitski nodded stiffly but she didn't respond.

She looked a little like his niece, he thought, his brother's eldest daughter. He'd noticed that right away. Not a lot, but a little. They had the same coloring and they both had that same sad look around the eyes.

He had no idea where his niece had gotten that look but it had been there as long as he remembered.

When they pulled away out of the driveway Covitski looked at her again and she was turning in the other direction. Away from them.

Thirty-nine

It was early. There was no one on the street. He passed the Roberts house and considered stopping in.

He heard the dog barking.

He passed Ed Schorr's place where the car with the two dead cops was parked and would be parked for quite a long time and then the Crocker place and he was almost to the house where the twins lived, he didn't know their names or the names of their parents because they were relatively new there, when he saw one of the two spinsters across the street come out with a bag of garbage.

He guessed she was an early riser.

He pointed the magnum and fired.

The woman went down with a big red hole in her apron and the sound was huge and he guessed that would wake up the neighborhood all right, people would be locking their doors pretty soon and he'd better get on this right away.

He walked up the porch to the house where the twins lived and opened the door and saw the little boy coming through the living room in his pyjamas rubbing the sleep from his eyes and he shot him once in the head with the .38. He walked down a hall to a bedroom. The man and woman were startled and they were just now getting out of bed.

The woman put her hands in front of her face when she saw the gun so he shot her in the stomach. The man hunched down trying to hide behind the bed. He walked over and shot the man once in one leg and once in the other leg. The man squirmed and cried out so he shot him in the chest and then walked out of the bedroom down the hall through the living room and out the door.

He heard the little girl, the other twin, saying mommy mommy somewhere back behind him.

The spinster's sister was bent down over her body on the lawn. She was crying and shaking her as though she were trying to wake her. He didn't want to use the magnum. There were so few bullets. He shot her in the back with the .38 instead and then crossed the street and over across the lawn and even though he was pretty sure she was dead he shot her in the head for good measure.

He jogged down that side of the street, the side opposite his house, past the Crocker, Schorr, and Roberts places and past his own house and the Murdoch place on this side of the street to the house where the Leigh kids lived, the ones who had stolen the pickets off his fence. He walked up to the porch and tried the door and since it was locked he used the magnum. The magnum punched a hole in the door two inches wide and the lock was gone completely. Its roar moved away from him down the street like a raw wind. He had four rounds left.

He opened the door and walked inside. He listened. The house was silent. He heard a noise upstairs, something moving so he climbed the stairs. The noise was coming from a closet in one of the bedrooms so he walked in and fired through the closet and then he opened the door. The older of the two boys slumped out across his feet wearing nothing but a pair of briefs. The boy was still alive. He stepped back and aimed carefully and shot him.

He heard someone running down the hall and into the next bedroom. He trotted out the door and saw that Leigh, the father, and the younger boy had opened the bedroom window. The boy was already out on the sloped shingled roof trying to work his way down but the father was only halfway out the window. He waited until the father got both legs over the windowsill and then shot him in the back and watched him tumble off the roof onto the cracked white sidewalk below. He heard the boy screaming, down on all fours, trying to cling to the roof and looking back at him. He left him there and went back to the stairs and down.

The woman was on the phone in the kitchen and he knew it was the police she was trying to call. He shot her once in the face and she fell across the breadboard and he hung up the phone.

He walked outside. He didn't know how many bullets were left in the clip so he popped it and tossed it on the curb and inserted another.

He crossed the street.

He saw a car coming down the road and waited and watched standing on the sidewalk under a tree until the car pulled by gliding past him and then turned and tracked the car with the magnum. When he fired he saw the back window shatter and glass explode out of the windshield and saw the vivid splash of blood across what was left of it as the car went over the curb and into a tree across the street in front of Bobby Dimmit's house who he had known all his life since he was just a boy. He had no idea if the driver was a man or if it was a woman.

There were three rounds left in the magnum.

He walked up the steps to Roberts' house.

The dog was barking. He looked through the window but he couldn't see the dog. He tried the door but it was locked. He shot at the lock with the magnum.

He tried the door again but either the lock had somehow held against all expectation or there were other locks he couldn't see. He fired a little higher and tried the door again. Nothing.

There was only one round left in the magnum.

He decided to let it go at that. Roberts was a busybody. At some point when he thought it was safe to do so Roberts would stick his head up in one of the windows and he could use the .38.

He could hear the Leigh boy up on the roof still crying and screaming. He walked to the Schorr house.

There were sirens in the distance. He would have to make it fast.

He knew this house. He had played here as a kid with whatsisname who had moved to Delaware or something and the back door was practically paper.

He went around back watching Roberts' window just in case and then turned and went around the sloping padlocked trapdoor entrance to Schorr's cellar, stepped over a garden hose and went to the door. He opened the screen. He didn't even bother to see if the door was locked. He just kicked it in and walked inside into the kitchen and there was Schorr standing there with a knife in his hand from the open drawer.

He really didn't mind Schorr and was annoyed to find him there. Schorr was efficient at the post office and he had a pleasant manner. But it annoyed him so much that the man was in his way now because it was his wife he was really after that he shot him in the right leg with the .38 and then when he went down placed the gun to his temple and fired again, brains and blood all over his pants leg and shoes, and walked past him through the kitchen.

She was hiding behind the couch in the living room.

Ohmygodpleasedon't she said like it was all one word.

When he shot her the first time she moved and tried to fling herself away, so that instead of hitting her in the chest the bullet caught her in the throat and it was probably the bloodiest thing he'd ever seen, her trying to stop it up with her slippery hands. He shot her in the heart. The blood pumping from her neck began to ebb.

The sirens were much closer and it sounded like there were a lot of them so he knew he had to hurry, so he went out past Schorr's body through the back door and jogged around past Roberts' house where the dog was still barking like it could smell the blood in the air and was going completely crazy now around to the front of his house and through the picket gate.

He heard cars screech to a halt their sirens still going to the right and to the left of him in the street in front of his house and he threw the door shut

behind him and threw the locks, slapped the clip out of the .38 and reached
into his pocket for another.

He was home.

Among friends.

In his fortress.

It was the very best day of his life.

Forty

The squad cars and ambulances were all over the street like flies on shit parked in front of the house all the way up and down the street and Rule was on the bullhorn.

Lock was at the front window, or near the window, being careful not to show himself.

'I don't like that . . . goddamn thing there!' he yelled. 'I don't want you to use that anymore. You want to talk to me, you use the telephone!'

Okay. You got it, he thought. He turned to Covitski.

'The shooters in place?'

Covitski nodded. 'Both doors, every window.'

He went to his car.

'Patch me through to an open line,' he said. 'And get me Lock.'

It took a moment and then he heard it ringing. Lock picked up on the second ring.

'Hello.'

'Hello, Wayne.'

'This is Wayne. What's the last name of the party you want to speak to?'

'Lock.'

'Okay. Who are you and what do you want?'

'My name's Rule. I'm just outside here. How are things going in there, Wayne?'

'Fine.'

'Are you all alone?'

'I have a Mrs Carole Gardner in here with me and a Mr Edwards.'

'And how are they doing?'

'They're dying. Dead. I don't know.'

'Which?'

'I said I don't know.'

'It's pretty important, Wayne.'

'I said I don't know.'

'Okay. Is there anything you need? Anything we can do for you?'

'No.'

'How about them? Mr Edwards and Mrs Gardner, I mean. They'll need a doctor, right?'

'They're fine.'

'You said they were hurt.'

'They're fine. No doctor.'

'You've been pretty busy tonight.'

'I know.'

'So why don't you come outside – leave the guns in there – come on out and we'll talk about it. I bet you've got a lot to say, Wayne, and I'll tell you, I'd really be interested to hear.'

'Oh sure.'

'I mean it. No one's going to hurt you if you do. You have my word on it. We'll just talk. That's all.'

'What's your name again?'

'Rule.'

'I don't know you, do I?'

'I don't think so. I don't think we've ever met.'

'You're with the police.'

'That's right. I'm a Lieutenant with the Barstow police.'

'Lieutenant Rule.'

'That's right.'

There was a pause on the line.

'Listen,' he said. 'I'm kinda busy right now. I'll have to talk to you later, okay? 'Bye.'

He hung up.

Busy with what? Rule wondered. If Gardner and Edwards were already dead.

'Well?'

Covitski was at his side leaning into the car.

'He won't say if they're dead or not but they're in there and you can at least figure they're hurting. This guy talks like I'm trying to sell him a subscription to *Better Home and Gardens*. No affect at all.'

'No what?'

'Affect. His voice. It's flat. Totally flat.'

'He's not scared.'

'No. He's not.'

'Did he say what he wants?'

Rule shrugged. 'He doesn't want anything.'

Covitski thought about it.

'You're gonna try him again, right?'

'Yeah. Let's give him a minute, though. I don't want to push him.'

He glanced over his shoulder. A few houses down they were hauling a

169

boy up through a window off the edge of a roof. A pair of uniforms were leading Roberts and his dog to the police line down the block away from there. The dog seemed stunned by all the activity. For once it wasn't barking.

He took a cigarette off Covitski and lit his own from its tip.

'Weird what you think of,' he said and handed it back to him.

'What?'

If Howard Gardner had left his wife alone we wouldn't be here.'

Covitski gave him a look. Like he ought to have his head examined.

'We'd be here, Joe,' he said. 'Sooner or later. We'd be here.'

Forty-one

'They want me to go outside,' said Wayne. 'What do you think?'

They didn't answer.

It wasn't fair. He'd been alone all his fucking life making every decision for himself and here he was just asking for a little advice and it was exactly like living with his mother, they were there but they weren't there.

'What do you think, dammit?' he said.

They said nothing.

He was writing down their response to him or lack of it in his notebook and dating it carefully when the phone rang. He finished writing. *RETAL*. Then he got up and got it.

Forty-two

She had to use the bathroom.

Her feet were bare on the rug and her legs were very heavy as she slid them down and she was wet, something on her head was wet and she was wet all down her face and down across her body. She had to go to the bathroom and he was on the phone, talking, his back to her, he was a strange dark blur moving against the white wall that tilted oddly as she rose off the couch and trotted unsteadily barefoot down the hall, using the walls on both sides for support and to keep her balance and feeling giddy, drunk, wanting to laugh and wondering when had she been drinking? And then she was in the kitchen, not the bathroom, there was no bathroom here oh hell she was in the wrong room but she saw the door in front of her and something told her she should probably no definitely use it.

She turned the knob but the door wouldn't open.

It was stuck.

It was locked.

That was the problem. The door was locked. And here it was – here was the lock. A little anchor-shaped thing made of brass. She turned it.

It was still locked.

There was a button on the doorknob and you had to turn it button button who's got the button so she did and turned the knob again and pulled open the door and almost fell down sick to her stomach there on the steps, giddiness turned to nausea the moment the warm morning breeze hit her face and the sun hit her eyes, a warm blinding slap across the face, and she saw the mowed lawn like a hazy drifting sea in front of her and behind it the sparse row of hedges, and someone in the hedges – a man – said Oh my God.

The man was blurry too but as he stepped out of the hedges she saw the rifle he carried and knew what it was, a grey-white glint of metal in the sunlight and the rifle spoke to her clearly and the rifle said run.

RUN!

She stumbled on the third step but then she was on the lawn up and running lurching along the side of the house, her bare feet on the grass wet with dew, breeze across her body, realizing her dress was open the *man had seen her and clutching it together with one hand and flailing at the hedges with the other because she had somehow stumbled into the hedges and they seemed to want to slap her down so she pushed them away. Go away. Go away you. Running.* The man with the gun *was not going to reach her. She would not let him reach her. He was not going to catch her. Oh no. Not again.*

She saw the row of cars ahead of her on the street and she ran toward the cars but the man was getting near her oh God *he was near and she screamed in panic. She screamed again as she felt his fingers clutch at her arm and then slip off again. The wetness was all over her now running down her all across her body and the dress was open but she didn't care and she screamed again and fell against the hedges her hands scraping the hard picket fence behind it as the fingers reached out and grabbed her, closed on her arm. Those hard calloused fingers on that enormous evil hand that was a man's hand. He had her.*

The man with the gun.

He had her.

Had her over and over again like a film on a loop. Over and over.

And then the world exploded.

Forty-three

Rule saw the door open and Wayne in the doorway and heard the magnum roar as the patrolman who had finally reached Carole Gardner slammed back against the picket fence and fell, his shoulder sprayed like mud across the clean white birch, and as he ducked down behind the hood of the car and they opened fire he was aware that Wayne was yelling something, his mouth was open and the lips were moving while he stood in the doorway firing the .38, standing legs spread wide and then jerking with the impact of the bullets but still standing and still firing.

He saw Carole fall sideways to her knees, then sprawl out onto the grass. And he thought, She's shot! Jesus! *Us or him?* After everything else. After a night he could only imagine.

He felt his stomach slide.

He ducked low around the car and began to run.

He knew it would be just like this.

No pain. He felt nothing but impact as the bullets hit him, a shower of tiny meteors, celestial bodies flattening against him pouring through him as he ascended through the weighty morning sunlight into the thinner nighttime sky that lay above. He knew that he'd been kind to them. To all those people who owed him their own ascendency now.

He hadn't meant to be kind. That was not the idea.

It was an irony that there was so much pleasure.

He didn't mind. He forgave them all in a way.

All the insects who had ever stung him.

Bless you.

He screamed out his love for Carole Gardner. *I love you I love you I love you!* he screamed again and again even though he doubted she could hear him over the gunfire.

He meant it.

Meant it even as he turned the gun on her and fired through the storm of bees the driving hailstones bringing her the gift as the bullets tiny comets slammed home into his body.

She'd shown him the way.

174

And as the man approached her he fired once again, at him this time, at the man, and saw him raise his gun and knew in an instant how accurate the shot would be, sighted the trajectory of the man's bullet even before it left the chamber. He knew it would be a perfect shot, an admirable shot, pinning him there to the door like a butterfly to paper right between the eyes.

This man too he loved.

I was born to love, he thought. *Just this way*. His final thought before the bullet proved true to its word and Wayne rested.

The street was a hall of echoes.

It smelled like the Fourth of July.

The bullet had passed through the meat of his arm just below his shoulder and exited through the other side. He wouldn't be able to lift her. He didn't try.

He stayed on his knees and waited for Covitski and the paramedics.

He felt for a pulse.

He gazed down at her face, saw where the towels had slipped away and the soft-looking wound and realized suddenly that she didn't look remotely similar to Ann. It wasn't the wound or the blood disguising her. She never had. He wondered how or why he had ever thought so in the first place.

Situational, he thought. A resemblance that was strictly situational. Abused women. Drunken husbands.

Had he ever thought otherwise?

The thought that he might have suddenly bothered him.

He couldn't find a pulse.

Was that why he felt like crying?

'Rule. Can you stand up? Come on. Stand up with me. Let the boys here do their jobs, Joe. Come on.'

Covitski had his arm. He looked up and saw that he was surrounded by paramedics. They had the stretcher ratcheted down and were ready to lift her onto it but he was preventing them from doing so. He was gripping her wrist like his life depended on it.

It was no way to feel for a pulse.

He let her go.

'Sorry,' he said.

And he had no idea at that moment – whether it was Covitski or the paramedics or Carole Gardner – exactly who he was saying that to.

THURSDAY

Forty-four

'What time is it?' she said.

Rule looked at his watch. 'Nearly noon. Welcome.'

It didn't feel like noon. Noon was supposed to be hot and the room was cold. There was too much air conditioning. Of course there was. She was in the hospital.

The room seemed to darken suddenly. A shadow falling.

She ran her tongue across dry cracked lips.

'What day?'

'Thursday. You've been out for over twenty-four hours. You have a concussion. He shot you once in the right thigh. Once in the hip. They removed the bullets and you're going to be just fine.'

'What . . . what happened?' she said.

'We got him,' he said. 'It's over.'

'You've been here . . .?'

'Only the past couple of hours. I had to get this taken care of.' He smiled and raised his arm and she saw the sling and the bone-white cast. 'They just turned me loose, actually.'

'And . . . Lee . . .?'

He looked at her and she realized she'd known all along. Maybe because he wasn't there sitting in a chair next to Rule beside the bed. And maybe, more probably, because of the feeling she'd awoken with, that had flung itself over her like one final rape immediately upon waking – that sense of loss she'd felt, that feeling of being somehow linked to him that had come too late, too deeply and far too late, stunned that somehow this link too had been taken from her before she had even fully realized the depth of it and that now he was gone. No perfect partner. Insane as she had been back then perhaps and certainly wrong as she had been. A deep black hole they had dug for themselves but it was their hole dug for their reasons. He had been her lover. Her friend.

The feel of his hands. The smell of him. The easy silences.

They were friends.

'I'm sorry,' he said.

And he *was* sorry. It wasn't just something you said to somebody. It

179

wasn't just formality. She could see that he meant it. She thought that he was probably a very good man. And she had been lying to him forever now.

She thought that he would understand the tears.

'I want you to know something,' he said. His voice was soft, gentle. 'I want you to listen to me.

'This man Lock, he had it in for you. He murdered your husband.

'We don't know why and it doesn't matter why. Lock was crazy.

'We can place him at the murder site.

'Then he kidnapped you and Lee.

'I want you to know that there is no one who connects you to any of these killings. No one blames you for anything. Not the families of the victims and not the police. You understand that? When they let you out of here you'll be free to go. You'll have to make a statement, a pretty detailed statement, but after that you'll be free. You understand, Carole?'

She hesitated. Were it not Rule sitting here telling her this, were it anybody else she would not have believed it possible.

She looked at him and nodded. He reached for a tissue on the night stand beside her and handed it across to her.

'Why,' she said. 'Why are you . . .?'

He stopped her.

'Say it's because I believe you've been a victim here all along. No, let me correct that. I don't believe it, I know it. We both do. You should try to remember that about yourself. A victim will do some crazy things to stop being a victim and maybe you did too. But that doesn't make you crazy, and it doesn't make you evil.

'So don't ask why. When you get out of here just get on with it. *Just get on with your life.* Be free.'

He looked away. There was pain in his eyes.

She glimpsed it there just before he turned away.

She did not think it was his wounded arm.

They sat in silence for a while. As though something awkward had just happened between them.

'I've got an appointment,' he said finally.

He rose slowly from the chair.

'I'll be back to see you tomorrow, all right? We'll talk. Is there anything you need? Anything I can get for you?'

'Thanks. Not right now,' she said.

He turned and walked to the door.

'Oh God!' she said. 'The cats. Beast and Vinni.'

He laughed. 'Vinni. *That's* her name. I remembered the other one's. I meant to tell you. I hope you don't mind. I just sort of . . . *adopted* them. Had my partner bring them over to the house. Just for the duration.'

She found that she could smile.

It almost surprised her that she was able to smile.

'I'm grateful,' she said. 'Thank you. Thank you for everything.'

He nodded. And for a moment she saw the look in his eyes again as he turned and walked out the door and she thought, *So much pain. It was everywhere.*

Even in this man who was so kind.

She leaned back into the softness of the pillow. The room was still.

Perhaps she'd sleep. She'd try to sleep.

It was good for her.

It occurred to her that it was possible that she would dream of Lee. Of Lee and not Howard nor Wayne nor any man who had hurt her. She did not believe she would dream of them now. But of him, perhaps.

She thought that it would break her heart to wake up knowing she had dreamt of Lee but it was perhaps a way to thank him and it was a way to remember.

It was so strange that for the first time since she was a little girl she really wanted to remember.

The bed was soft. She settled in.

Forty-five

'So,' Marty said. 'You saved the Maiden.'

'Please. Don't start,' said Rule.

'Well you did, didn't you? And you got the bad guy?'

'Yeah. I did.'

'There. See? Glad to hear it.'

'I'll tell you something,' Rule said. 'I sat there in the hospital looking at her while she was still under and you know what? I realized something.

'All this time I've been thinking that Carole reminded me of Ann, situation-wise certainly, and even looks-wise, and that was why it was getting to me, that was why I was having so much trouble with this one and why I was thinking of Ann all the time. But it wasn't that. It wasn't Carole Gardner reminding me of Ann.

'It was Wayne reminding me of *me*. How about that?'

Marty didn't comment.

He sat back heavily in the chair. 'Me and Wayne,' he said. 'You see what I'm getting at? It's what we do. We *hurt things*. Not just by being. Not just by walking through life. Everybody does that. You can't help but do that.

'But by being *who we are*.'

'Hey Joe. That's a pretty damn big stretch. You're not some killer.'

'No, of course not. But I destroy things. Faith. Trust. Connections. Lives, in a way, or parts of lives. Because of *who* I am and *what* I am.

'Me and Wayne.'

Marty studied him a moment.

'There's a difference,' he said.

'Sure. I don't go around blowing people away on the highway.'

'I don't mean that. What I mean is that a guy like this Wayne character, he puts nothing back into it, does he? He just takes. You? You do what you can to even things up, maybe even tip the scales a little back toward something positive. Something decent. You do your job. You do what you can.

'You save the Maiden.'

'You think that's enough? I don't. I can't.'

'Listen to me. It's a damn rough piece of business living in the world. Nothing's *ever* enough. The point is not to give up on it. To do what you *can* do. You haven't destroyed Ann's life or Chrissie's life for Godsakes. Sure you've changed them. And maybe not wholly for the best either because it didn't work out for the best.

'But you think about it – they've gotten to know a pretty decent guy. That counts for something.' He laughed. 'There aren't all that many of us around, you know? You're not dead yet. And neither is she. Lives have a way of getting richer if they don't stop happening altogether.'

'That which doesn't kill me makes me stronger, huh?'

'Something like that, yeah.'

'You think you're a pretty hot ticket, don't you Marty?'

'Yeah. I do, Joe.' He sat back in the chair and lit a cigarette. He was breaking his own rule about smoking in session.

Rule guessed it counted as a special occasion.

'Don't you?' he said.

At home he fed the cats and called them both by name, petted them when they were finished and followed them into the living room and scratched their ears and looked at the telephone. He did the dishes in the sink and looked down the hall to the telephone and thought about what time it was in California. He left the tv off for a change so that the house was quiet.

He sat down in the living room with a beer in his hand and the cats came by again wanting to be scratched and petted, rubbing up against him, so he obliged them. They began roughhousing, playing. He watched them. The cats didn't need him anymore. They had each other.

He was left to his own devices.

He got up and walked to the telephone and picked up the receiver and held it a moment and then put it back in the cradle.

He thought, Not now.

He turned on the outside light and walked out to the garage in the cooling night.

The dolls' house was painted white with black shutters. He had done a good job on it so far and it welcomed him as his own house had not aside from the cats and he bent to the tasks remaining – cutting this and building that, making something, shaping something, finishing something, doing what he could do.